"Hunter, please help me make sense of this," she said, her voice shaking.

"There is no sense to make of it," he replied tersely. Damn it, who was doing this to her? And why? The box implied a threat even though no note was included.

He turned back to find her looking at him. She looked so small. Her eyes were filled with fear, and as she reached up to tuck a strand of hair behind her ear, her fingers trembled.

He took her hand in his and pulled her down to the sofa. He sat next to her. Even though he was on duty, there was no way he could just walk away and leave her so frightened.

He wanted to hold her through the night if that was as long as it took to make her fear ease.

"Ainsley, I swear I'm going to do everything in my power to get to the bottom of all this."

STALKER IN
THE SHADOWS

New York Times Bestselling Author
CARLA CASSIDY

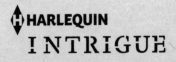

⬧HARLEQUIN
INTRIGUE

HARLEQUIN®
INTRIGUE®

ISBN-13: 978-1-335-40163-2

Stalker in the Shadows

Copyright © 2021 by Carla Bracale

Harlequin Enterprises ULC
22 Adelaide St. West, 40th Floor
Toronto, Ontario M5H 4E3, Canada
www.Harlequin.com

Printed in U.S.A.

Carla Cassidy is an award-winning, *New York Times* bestselling author who has written over 150 novels for Harlequin. In 1995, she won Best Silhouette Romance from *RT Book Reviews* for *Anything for Danny*. In 1998, she won a Career Achievement Award for Best Innovative Series from *RT Book Reviews*. Carla believes the only thing better than curling up with a good book to read is sitting down at the computer with a good story to write.

Books by Carla Cassidy

Harlequin Intrigue

Desperate Strangers
Desperate Intentions
Desperate Measures
Stalked in the Night
Stalker in the Shadows

Scene of the Crime

Scene of the Crime: Bridgewater, Texas
Scene of the Crime: Bachelor Moon
Scene of the Crime: Widow Creek
Scene of the Crime: Mystic Lake
Scene of the Crime: Black Creek
Scene of the Crime: Deadman's Bluff
Scene of the Crime: Return to Bachelor Moon
Scene of the Crime: Return to Mystic Lake
Scene of the Crime: Baton Rouge
Scene of the Crime: Killer Cove
Scene of the Crime: Who Killed Shelly Sinclair?
Scene of the Crime: Means and Motive

Visit the Author Profile page at Harlequin.com.

CAST OF CHARACTERS

Ainsley Meadows—A woman filled with dark secrets and trying to make a new start.

Hunter Churchill—Deputy sheriff. When Ainsley's secrets are revealed, will he love her or lock her up?

Peter Waverly—Will his hunt for Ainsley wind up in a deadly reunion?

Jimmy Miller—Is the rejected cowboy angry enough to want revenge?

Ben Wilkins—This unpredictable man has a grudge against Ainsley. Has his grudge turned deadly?

Chapter One

"Ainsley, order up," Eddie Burwell, aka Big Ed, called from the pass-through window between the kitchen and the dining area of the Dusty Gulch Café.

Ainsley Meadows hurried to the window to pick up her order. "Hmm, looks good, Big Ed," she said of the day's special of an open-face hot roast beef sandwich with a special slaw on the side.

Big Ed flashed his wide, toothless grin in response. He told everyone he had gotten rid of his teeth to better taste the food he cooked. But the rumor was he'd really lost his teeth in a bar fight years ago when he'd been young and courting the wrong side of the law.

She carried the order to Jim Nelson, one of her regulars. Jim was an attractive older man with snow-white hair and a sweet disposition. She always enjoyed waiting on him.

"Here you go, Mr. Nelson," she said as she placed the plate before him. "Can I get you more coffee?"

"Not right now," he replied. "You always take good care of me when I come in."

"I try," she replied with a smile.

She definitely tried to do the best job she could as a waitress here at the Dusty Gulch Café. She was hoping to make the small Kansas town her forever home.

When Big Ed, who not only cooked for the café but was also the owner, had hired her as a waitress, he had quickly learned she was alone with her eight-year-old daughter. They were stranded in town with car trouble and had no place to stay. So he'd offered her the apartment in the back of the café, which had been emptied by his daughter when she'd left town a couple of years ago.

Ainsley had been thrilled with the accommodations and considered it her first real bit of luck in a very long time. She'd been in town for two and a half months now, and she prayed that finally she and her daughter, Melinda, would be safe here, that this was finally the place where they could put down roots and not live in fear.

The noon rush had just passed when fellow waitress Lana Kincaid sidled up to Ainsley at the coffee machine. "Don't look now, but your man just walked in."

Ainsley flashed a quick glance over her shoulder to the café's front door, where Deputy Sheriff Hunter Churchill had just entered.

She quickly looked back at the older waitress. "He's not my man," she protested even as her heartbeat quickened at the sight of him.

"He wants to be," Lana replied and then cackled. "Trust me, I've been through four marriages. I know when a man has the hots for a woman, and that man definitely has the hots for you."

"Stop it," Ainsley protested. "I think the coffee fumes you inhale all day long have made you delusional," she added with a laugh of her own. Still, if Ainsley was honest with herself, she'd confess she had a bit of a crush on the handsome deputy.

When she turned around and saw the deputy seated in one of her booths, she couldn't help the warmth that filled her cheeks.

She pulled her order pad from her apron pocket and approached the booth. "Good afternoon, Deputy Churchill," she greeted him.

"Afternoon, Ainsley. How's my favorite waitress doing today?" His deep green eyes seemed to smile at her just before his lips curved into the gesture.

"I don't know, I'll have to ask Lana how she's doing," she replied teasingly.

He laughed. "Oh no. Don't even mention my name to that man-eating woman. I have no desire to be her husband number five."

"I'll do my best try to protect you from her," she replied with a grin.

Deputy Hunter Churchill's rich dark hair was short and neat, and his features were classically sculpted. He was tall and lean and broad shouldered. He wore his khaki uniform with a confidence that instantly portrayed strength and only added to his overwhelming attractiveness.

He'd been playfully flirtatious with her since the

first time she'd waited on him, and it had only been recently that she felt comfortable enough to tease and flirt back a little.

"What can I get for you today?" She looked down at her order pad. Even with all the different odors in the room—the frying onions and hot coffee, the baking meats and aromatic sauces—she could still smell his enticing, slightly spicy, slightly woodsy cologne.

"How's the special?" he asked.

She gazed at him once again and smiled. "We've had lots of orders for the special and so far no complaints."

"So, what you're telling me is nobody has died from eating the special today." He grinned again, and the temperature in the room seemed to shoot up a hundred degrees.

She laughed. "That's exactly right."

"Okay, then, I'll take the roast beef with a regular soda," he replied.

"I'll be right back with your soda." She hurried away from the booth, put his order in and then went to the soda machine. As she drew his drink, she released a deep breath.

Hunter was the first man in years who made her remember she was a twenty-nine-year-old single woman who had been alone for a long time.

Is it safe? The familiar words jumped into her mind. They were words that had haunted her for a little over three years. She hoped it was safe to make a home here in Dusty Gulch.

It was important for her daughter that they put down real roots and try to build a normal life without fear. Deep in her heart, she wasn't even sure that was possible.

She shoved these troubling thoughts aside and hurried back to Hunter's booth to deliver the drink. "Here we go," she said as she put the glass in front of him.

"Thanks. How's your day going?" he asked.

"Good, what about you? Are you catching all the bad guys in Dusty Gulch?"

He laughed. "Right now the bad guys have all been fairly quiet…just the way we like it."

"That's good. Uh…let me just go check on your food order."

"Ainsley, before you go, I was just wondering if you ever go out on your days off or in the evenings after work?"

"In the couple of months that I've been in town, nobody has asked me out," she replied, her heart quickening by the spark in his eyes.

"What if somebody did? Would you be interested in going out?"

"It would depend on who was asking," she replied with a teasing smile.

"What if I'm asking? Would you be interested in maybe going out to dinner someplace else on your night off? And of course your daughter is invited."

Is it safe? It's just a dinner out. The two voices whispered in her head. Surely it was safe after all this time. "I'd be interested, but not with Melinda," she replied. Her cheeks warmed with a blush.

She'd never really thought about dating, but she definitely didn't want to invite her daughter into spending time with some random guy Ainsley went out to dinner with.

Hunter smiled. "Great, so when is your next night off?" The man had a gorgeous grin that involved not only his lips, but every other muscle in his face. It was a smile that welcomed you in, one that warmed the person it was directed at.

"Ainsley?"

"Ainsley, order up," Big Ed yelled.

She flushed, realizing she'd been staring at Hunter in silence for too long. "Thursday," she said. "I'm off on Thursdays."

"Do you like Chinese?"

"I love it," she replied.

"Then how about I pick you up Thursday around five and we'll go to the Red Wok and over dinner we can get to know each other."

"Ainsley," Big Ed hollered again.

"That sounds good," she replied. "And now if I don't pick up your order, Big Ed is going to have a heart attack." She hurried away from the booth with the sound of Hunter's deep, pleasant rumble of laughter warming her.

Once he'd been served, she continued to wait on the patrons that continued to trickle in, but in the back of her mind she thought about the date with Hunter that would occur in two days.

She'd never really considered what life might look like if they ever managed to settle in somewhere. Working at the café she'd met a lot of the Dusty Gulch natives, and for the most part she'd enjoyed her interaction with all of them.

However, she'd never thought ahead enough to see herself in a position to make real friends or to date anyone. And now a handsome deputy had asked her out.

Of all the people she could choose to hang out with, anyone in law enforcement would be the last she would pick. If she didn't play things right, he could be very dangerous to her.

Still, she couldn't help that something about Hunter Churchill drew her. Besides the fact that she found him drop-dead gorgeous, there was something in the very depths of his green eyes that pulled her in, that made her want to get to know him better.

It was a whisper of pain and Ainsley knew all about pain…both the physical and the emotional kind. It was that pain that had forced her to make decisions she'd never dreamed she would have to make.

As she thought about her date with Hunter, there was both an excitement and a sadness inside her. She was excited to spend time with him and get to know him better. And the sadness came from knowing she was going to lie to him about who she was and where she'd come from.

The faint stir of misery came from the fact that everything about her was a complete lie, from the color of her hair to her very name.

HUNTER LEANED BACK at his desk in the Dusty Gulch police station. There were only five large desks in the room, shared by a total of fourteen deputies. Sheriff Wayne Black's private office was behind a closed glass door just in back of the five deputies' desks.

Lanie Byrant was the first person anyone interacted with when they came into the station. She was a charming brunette with sparkling blue eyes and met everyone who came in with a problem with dignity and respect. She was also the gatekeeper between the public and the officers.

Although Hunter found the twenty-three-year-old attractive, he'd never had a romantic interest in her. Instead she was more like a little sister to him.

That was the sum of the Dusty Gulch police force, and over the past two months they had been stretched thin with the murder of an old man while he slept and the sensational story of terror and attempted murder among the powerful and wealthy Albright family.

Thankfully things were back to normal with the usual crimes of speeding, stealing, mischief and public intoxication. It was as if the winds of September had blown away the evil that had possessed some of the town people in the month of August.

Hunter looked up from a report he'd been writing as the door opened and Deputy Nick Marshall walked in.

"Hey, buddy," he greeted as he sat at the desk across from Hunter. "What's happening?"

Nick and Hunter were the only two single men on the force. They had grown up together on neighboring farms. Nick was thirty four years old, two years older than Hunter and one of his closest friends.

"I'm just finishing writing up a report about Ben Wilkins being drunk and disorderly last night in front of the grocery store," Hunter said.

"I thought he'd moved to Makenville," Nick replied, referring to a small town about twenty miles away from Dusty Gulch.

"Yeah, well he's back. He's living in the motel and supposedly looking for a job."

Nick shook his head. "With his reputation for drinking, he's going to have trouble finding any work."

Hunter leaned forward. "So, ask me what else is new."

"What else is new?"

"This Thursday I have a date with Ainsley." Hunter couldn't help but smile.

"Ah, you lucky dog," Nick replied. "I was thinking about asking her out, but I had the distinct feeling if I did she'd turn me down."

Hunter's smile fell as he looked at his friend. "Ah man, I'm sorry. I didn't know you were even interested in her."

Nick laughed. "A new gorgeous single woman moves to town? I imagine every single man in Dusty

Gulch is interested, but she said yes to you. I hope you aren't planning on taking her to the café."

It was Hunter's turn to laugh. "I doubt she'd be happy with me if I took her to the place where she works all the time. Actually, I'm taking her to the Red Wok."

"Seriously man, I hope it goes well."

"Yeah, me too."

The two men visited for a few minutes longer, and then Nick left to go back out on the streets and Hunter finished up writing his report.

The rest of the workday passed peacefully, and finally Hunter was on his way home. Home was a three-bedroom ranch house he'd bought eight years ago. At that time he'd had his dream job and a beautiful wife. He'd been filled with happiness, and the future had looked so bright.

Those dreams had all shattered four years ago, leaving Hunter alone and with so many emotions to sort through. He'd been grieving and had become bitter and had isolated himself from everyone and everything.

A year ago he'd suddenly awakened to the fact that he was still young, that it wasn't too late to achieve the dreams he'd once had.

Ainsley was the first woman who had stirred something inside him, something that had been dormant for a very long time. Was she the right woman for him? He had no idea. Right now he just wanted to get to know her.

Physically he found her very attractive with her long

black hair and beautiful blue eyes. More than that, her smile warmed him in a way he hadn't felt with any other woman in town. Maybe it was because her smile seemed so open and her eyes shone with honesty.

He didn't know much about her. Her full name was Ainsley Meadows and she had a young daughter, but there had been no gossip about her to tell him anything else.

He wasn't expecting much of the date. It would be nice to find out if there could be something between them, something good and long-term. He was ready for that in his life. Of course, there was also the chance that the date could be a total bust and they would quickly realize they weren't right for each other.

He walked into his living room and was greeted by his black miniature schnauzer, Zeus. The little dog danced at his feet and then ran to the black recliner where Hunter usually sat and petted him.

"Okay, okay, I'm coming." Hunter laughed and sat. Zeus jumped up in his lap, and Hunter stroked down the dog's back. Zeus seemed to smile with utter happiness.

He remained there only a few minutes and then got up and opened the back door that led into the fenced backyard. Zeus darted outside.

About a year ago when his loneliness had become too heavy to bear, he'd found Zeus at the local shelter. At that time Zeus was only three months old and had been abandoned by a transient couple when they'd passed through town.

The dog had certainly brought Hunter a lot of joy, but there was still a core of loneliness inside him that yearned for somebody who could talk to him, somebody who might share his hopes and dreams.

Even though he knew it wasn't a good idea, he walked down the hallway and opened the door to the smallest bedroom. This room had once held a little boy's laughter and a toy box full of dreams.

It now held nothing except a photo on the wall, a crib and a teddy bear in a rocking chair to indicate that a little boy had lived two years of his life in the room.

Danny. His heart squeezed tight as he thought of that little boy…his son, who had died of childhood leukemia four years ago.

Hunter picked up the teddy bear and sank down in the rocking chair as memories of Danny took away all other thoughts. He'd handled his wife's betrayals and gotten past them. But this…this absence of the child he'd loved so much was another animal altogether. There were moments when it clawed at him, when it stabbed at his heart with a real, physical pain.

He'd grieved the loss of Danny all alone. His wife, Emily, had left him, but not before delivering one final devastation as she'd walked out of his life.

He raised the teddy bear to his nose and took a deep breath, imagining that he could still smell Danny's little-boy scent on the furry animal.

He remained that way for several long minutes and then finally stood and placed the teddy bear back in the chair. Before he left the room, he stared at the framed photo on the wall.

Danny had been a happy child, and the photo depicted a year-old Danny with Hunter. They were both laughing. Even though the disease had ravaged him, the little boy had remained a happy child who never complained.

And it was that particular spirit of Danny that Hunter now embraced. Danny would have wanted his daddy to be happy. As he left the room and closed the door behind him, he tucked his grief away, not to be entertained again until the next time he went into that bedroom.

He returned to the back door, where Zeus was waiting to come back inside. "Come on, boy." He opened the door, and Zeus greeted him all over again as if he hadn't seen Hunter a few minutes earlier.

Zeus had been Hunter's first step in reaching out for happiness once again. Now he was looking for more. He wanted to fall in love again, to get married and have children.

He just wanted to find an open and honest woman to share his dreams of home and family, and he was hoping that's what he would find with the new woman in town. He was desperately hoping Ainsley Meadows could be the new forever love in his life.

Chapter Two

Ainsley's nerves sizzled in her veins as she stood in the bathroom and spritzed on her favorite perfume. In fifteen minutes Hunter should show up for their date.

The Red Wok wasn't a dress-up kind of place, so she had on a pair of black skinny jeans and a long pink blouse that hugged her in all the right places.

Melinda had been picked up a few minutes before by Juanita Burwell, Big Ed's wife. The couple had five children, including an eight-year-old named Bonnie whom Melinda considered her very best friend in the whole world. Juanita had made it clear to Ainsley that Melinda was welcome in their house anytime. It was only one more thing that made Ainsley desperate to make this place her permanent home.

She left the bathroom and went into the small living room to await Hunter's arrival. Although she was excited about the night to come, in the past two days she'd changed her mind a dozen times about going out with him.

One part of her thought it was foolish to start a relationship when she didn't know if or when she might have to pick up and run. And then she reminded herself that it was just a simple meal out and nothing more.

It was exactly five o'clock when a knock fell on the door. A new burst of nerves shot through her as she answered. "Hi," Hunter greeted her.

For a brief moment she was speechless. Any time she'd ever seen him before, he had been in his khaki uniform. Now jeans hugged his long legs and a black polo shirt stretched across his broad shoulders and emphasized his slim waist and hips. He looked so handsome he nearly took her breath away.

His smile faltered slightly. "Ainsley, are you ready to go?"

"Yes…yes, I'm ready," she quickly answered. "Just let me grab my purse." Gosh, he probably thought there was something wrong with her when all she'd been doing was taking a brief moment to enjoy the view.

She grabbed her purse from the sofa and then went back to the door. "Now I'm ready." She closed and locked the door behind her.

His off-duty vehicle was a king-cab pickup truck. The inside was pristine clean and smelled of leather and the faint scent of his cologne.

"Are you hungry?" he asked once they were on their way.

"Definitely," she replied. "What about you?" Now that she was alone with him, she felt unaccountably shy.

He flashed her a quick smile. "I can always eat. So, how did you spend your day off?"

"The first thing I did was slept later than usual. It's always a luxury when I don't have to open the café at six in the morning."

"What else did you do?"

"Mostly fairly boring things, like laundry and cleaning." She released a small laugh. "If you're looking for me to tell you something exciting I did today, you're out of luck."

Once again he shot her one of his smiles. "Boring isn't all bad."

"What about you? How was your day?" she asked.

"Fairly boring," he replied, and they both laughed.

By that time they had arrived at the Red Wok. The restaurant had a cozy feel, and a pretty young waitress led them to a table for two. The air was redolent with the scents of exotic spices and simmering chicken and beef.

They were each given a menu and drink orders were taken and then the waitress left them. "One of my favorites is crab Rangoon," Hunter said. With the dim light in the restaurant and a candle flickering on the table, his eyes glowed with what appeared to be a preternatural light.

"I love them, too," Ainsley replied. "Anything deep-fried and filled with cream cheese is a winner in my book."

"So, besides a couple orders of crab Rangoon, what sounds good to you?"

She closed the menu and set it on the table. "I'm in the mood for sweet-and-sour chicken."

"Hmm, that sounds good, but I'm partial to General Tso's chicken. How about we make these specials so we get the soup and the appetizers with the meal?"

"That's fine with me."

The waitress served their drinks, took their orders and then left them alone once again. She returned a moment later with their soup.

Ainsley began to relax as they ate the soup and talked about favorite foods and cooking skills.

"I have to confess, my favorite kind of cooking mostly involves a microwave," he said. "But I do some pretty good work on my grill."

She laughed. "So, for the most part you're a zap-it kind of guy."

"For the most part, but I'll bet you're a good cook."

"I'm not a world-renowned chef, but I can hold my own," she replied. "Although I have to admit it's very easy to step out of the apartment and eat meals in the café. Big Ed lets me and my daughter eat for free, but the best part of that arrangement is there are never any dishes to clean up afterward."

"You cook but don't like to clean up dishes afterward, and I wouldn't mind doing dishes but don't really enjoy cooking. It sounds like we're a match made in heaven." He smiled at her, that devastating smile that half took her breath away.

Thankfully, at that moment the waitress appeared to serve their entrées and their orders of the crab Rangoon. "Tell me all about Ainsley Meadows," he said when the waitress had left.

"What do you want to know?" she asked. She picked up a piece of red pepper and popped it into her mouth. Now was the time she had to be on guard.

"Dusty Gulch isn't really a destination for anyone in the world, so what brought you here?"

"A flat tire," she replied with a small laugh. "After my divorce three years ago, I wanted a change of scenery, so my daughter and I were on a road trip to find a new place to live. As we were driving through Dusty Gulch I got a flat tire, and Mike, down at the garage, had to order a new tire, so we had to wait here for a couple of days. In those couple of days I realized this might be a nice place to live, and so here we are."

"Thank God for flat tires," he replied with a smile. "Where were you coming from originally?"

Let the lies begin, she thought with a touch of sadness. "A small town in Nevada." In truth she was from Portland, Maine.

"And your ex-husband was okay with you just taking off with his child?"

"He was an extremely uninvolved father and didn't really care where we went. I don't even know where he is now." Lie number two.

She shoved away any thoughts of her ex-husband, Peter, that tried to enter her mind. If she got caught up with thoughts of him, this night, this time with Hunter would be completely ruined.

"I'm sorry to hear that. I would give anything to be a husband and a father again," he replied.

She looked at him curiously. "Again? So you were married and have children?"

"No children, but I was married for about four years. But we divorced a little over four years ago." He took a bite of his dinner and then asked, "Do you want more children?"

She laughed. "To be honest I haven't given it much thought." She frowned. "If I found the right man and was married, I would maybe consider having more children. It would depend."

"Okay, now that those questions are out of the way, why don't you tell me what kinds of programs you like on television?"

The conversation grew less personal as they enjoyed the meal and talked about television and movies and music. It was a light, easy conversation that once again put her at ease.

She hoped Hunter didn't ask her any more questions that would require more lies. She liked him, and lying to him felt all wrong. But she couldn't tell him the truth—she couldn't tell anyone the truth about her past and the things she had done to survive.

If he knew the truth about her, Hunter would have to arrest her for breaking dozens of laws. But that wasn't the worst that would happen. She fought the shiver that threatened to race up her spine as she thought of the consequences of getting found by the man she had once married with such hopes of being loved for the rest of her life.

"Would you like something for dessert?" he asked.

"Goodness no, I'm absolutely stuffed." She wished she wanted dessert to prolong their time together.

"What do you think about parking on Main Street? We could take a leisurely walk together and maybe we'd work up our appetites for a visit to the ice cream parlor."

"That sounds nice." So, he wasn't in a hurry to end their time together, either. That warmed her in a way she hadn't been warmed in a long time.

They left the Red Wok, and he drove to the middle of Main Street, where they got out of the truck and began to walk. Within minutes he reached for her hand.

He had a big hand that swallowed hers in a pleasant grasp. She couldn't remember the last time a man had held her hand. It felt good, like a promise of something nice to come.

If he wanted to see her again, if he wanted to build something with her, could she allow it? There was a part of her that wanted it, but there was another part that told her it was foolish to continue to see him.

It was a beautiful September night, warm enough not to need a jacket or sweater. It was just after seven, and the people on the streets were starting to thin out.

Still, the people they passed greeted Hunter and offered friendly smiles to Ainsley. They talked about the various shops they passed, many of them Ainsley hadn't been in yet.

They finally came to the ice cream parlor. "Now could you eat some ice cream?" he asked.

"Maybe a cone."

He smiled. "Good, let's go inside."

Within minutes they were seated at one of the high round tables inside the shop. She had a chocolate ice cream cone in her hand, and he had a banana split.

"I have to confess, ice cream is one of my weaknesses," he said.

She smiled at him. "My daughter and I have been in here several times since we moved here. Ice cream is one of her weaknesses, too."

"Maybe sometime the three of us could come here together."

"Maybe," she replied. The idea that he saw them being together sometime in the future thrilled her more than it should. In fact, she liked Hunter more than she should.

He was funny and charming, and when he looked at her there was not only an interest, but also a bit of flame in the depths of his eyes that excited her, that made her feel pretty and desirable. He felt dangerous to her in a decidedly delicious way.

Once they'd eaten their ice cream, they headed back to her apartment. It was almost nine, and not only did she still have to go and pick up Melinda, she also had an early morning the next day in the café.

"Thank you, Hunter, for such a nice evening," she said once they stood in front of her apartment door at the back of the café.

"I really enjoyed it, Ainsley." He took a step closer to her, invading her personal space just a bit. "I'd like to see you again."

"I'd like that," she replied, half breathless with his nearness.

He smiled. "I'd also like to kiss you. May I do that?"

She was surprised and pleased that he respected her enough to ask her permission. She did not hesitate in giving him an answer.

"You may," she said and raised her face to him.

His mouth covered hers in a kiss that lasted long enough for her to know his lips were soft and warm. He didn't wrap his arms around her or pull her into him. It was just a sweet, soft kiss that, when it ended, made her want more.

He stepped back from her. "So, when can we do this again? Do you have any days off coming up?"

"I'm off on Sundays, but I reserve that day for time with my daughter. Other than that, I'm always off on Thursdays."

"What do you think about pizza?"

"I love pizza," she replied.

"Then how about next Thursday night I pick you up and we go to Antonio's Pizza? Same time as this evening?"

"That sounds good to me," she replied. Once again his eyes held that glow that warmed her from her head to her toes.

"In the meantime, I'll see you in the café."

She nodded. "Good night, Hunter."

"Good night, Ainsley."

She watched as he got into his truck and then pulled away. She went inside, shut the door and then leaned against it. She raised her fingers to her lips, remembering the thrill of Hunter's kiss.

There was a part of her that had hoped she wouldn't like him and the date would be a total bust. But that's not what happened.

She dug in her purse for her keys so she could run over to the Burwell residence to pick up Melinda. Minutes later as she drove across town, her thoughts lingered on Hunter.

Was it wrong for her to wish for a healthy relationship with a man? Was it wrong for her to be hungry for love in her life? A love she'd once hoped for but hadn't found in her first marriage?

Surely it was time for her to be able to breathe, to stop her constant vigilance and relax. It had been a little over a year since he'd last found her.

Enough time had passed that she was starting to feel safe for the first time since she'd escaped from him. But if she was wrong, if she somehow let down her guard and he found her again, she knew he would kill her and not break a sweat.

"TELL ME WHAT'S going on today, George." Hunter shot a quick look at Sheriff Wayne Black, who stood some distance away with his gun drawn, and then he looked back at the man who held a large butcher knife at his own throat.

George Calvert was a big man who suffered from chronic depression. He did pretty well when he was taking his meds, but Hunter could usually figure out how long he'd been off them by how dirty and how many stains rode his T-shirt.

They all stood in the front yard of George's attractive ranch house that was located only a block away from Hunter's own home.

As Hunter studied George's filthy shirt and greasy hair, he figured the man had been off his meds for a week to ten days. When he went off his meds, he medicated himself with booze, and it was evident now that George was drunk.

"I got nothing to live for," George said, tears streaming down his face.

"Come on, George, put the knife down and let's talk," Hunter replied. Although the sheriff stood ready to protect his deputy, Hunter was grateful he didn't try to interfere. Wayne didn't have a rapport with George like Hunter did.

"I'm not going to put the knife down. Just shoot me." He took an unsteady step forward and pointed the knife at Hunter. "Shoot me or I'm going to stab you."

Sheriff Black took a step forward, obviously concerned for Hunter's safety. "Come on, George. I'm not going to shoot you," Hunter replied, keeping his voice calm and steady. "Hell, George, I like you too much to shoot you."

George turned the knife back to his own neck. "I just need to die."

"Has Marybeth been around to see you?" Normally George's daughter kept a close eye on her father.

"She's gone…took the kids to visit their other grand-

eah, well, Zeus isn't very happy about me being
all night."

er gaze turned quizzical. "Zeus?"

My dog," he replied.

e laughed. "I was wondering why the god of thun-
nd lightning would be mad at you. I'll be back in
ute with your coffee."

nce again he was struck by her intelligence. He
ask a half a dozen women on the streets of Dusty
h who Zeus was, and they would probably think
as some kind of new dress designer.

e found himself even more curious about Ains-
background. As he thought back to their date the
before, he realized for the amount of time they'd
together, he'd really learned very little about her.
he only thing he really knew was that she was
nally from Nevada, divorced from an uncaring,
volved husband and father, and she loved crime
as and old rock and roll music.

ey hadn't really started to get into the meat of
other's lives yet, but hopefully that would all
n time. He smiled as she returned to his table
e coffeepot.

you know all about my morning, but I don't
ything about yours," he said as she filled his

e think…I served about twenty people for
double that for lunch and all I can think
half an hour or so I can take my break and
feet for just a few minutes." She gave him

parents in Kansas City." George looked even more mis-
erable. His knife hand trembled, and although Hunter
didn't fear the man would really cut his throat, he did
fear he might accidentally hurt himself.

"When is she coming home?" Hunter asked.

George frowned thoughtfully. "I think maybe tomorrow."

"Now, George, you know she wouldn't be happy to
find you like this. Why don't you drop the knife and
we'll go inside. You can get cleaned up, and I'll make
you a pot of coffee so you can sober up."

To Hunter's relief, he dropped the knife. Hunter
hurried forward and kicked the knife far enough away
that George couldn't pick it up again.

Hunter could have arrested George, but a little time
in jail wouldn't help this situation. So instead, for the
next forty-five minutes Hunter helped George get into
a shower and change into clean clothes. He found the
bottles of his medicine and got George to take it and
promise that he would take it again in the morning.

Hunter sat and drank a cup of coffee with the man,
then got him settled on the sofa so he could sleep it
off. Finally, as George began to snore, Hunter left the
house.

Depression was a crappy thing, he thought as he
headed back to the station. Hunter had definitely suffered situational depression when he'd lost his son, but
thankfully as time had passed and with a few counsel-
ing sessions, he'd managed to climb out of the darkness that had stolen all the joy from his life.

He had a couple more hours of work, and then he'd get to eat lunch and see Ainsley. After last night's date, he was really looking forward to spending more time with her.

He'd found her refreshingly authentic. She was also intelligent and funny and the type of woman he could see himself with for the long-term.

Of course all those were first-night impressions—they certainly needed to spend more time together and see how things went. Still, for the first time since his divorce, he was excited about the possibility of a relationship with a woman he found warm and exciting.

Although he'd wanted to wrap her up in his arms last night and give her a real, deep kiss, he'd restrained himself. Her lips had been so soft and incredibly hot. Kissing Ainsley again was definitely something he was looking forward to.

It was just after one when he entered the café. His gaze immediately found Ainsley taking orders from a group of four. He sat at one of the other tables that he knew she worked and waited for her to turn around and see him.

When she did, her lips curved into a smile that seemed like it was just for him alone, and her cheeks flushed with a charming shade of pink. God, she was so gorgeous.

She'd looked incredible the night before. He had been used to seeing her wearing the red-and-black apron that all of the waitresses wore. But last night

the pink blouse had hugged her curves had fit tight on her long, slender legs.

Within minutes she stood at the side heard you had an exciting few minutes talking down a man with a knife."

He looked at her in surprise. "Where that?"

"Sheriff Black was in here earlier e patience and great police work."

Hunter felt his cheeks warm as a wa rassment washed over him. "I was just d

"Maybe so, but according to Sheriff Bl above and beyond today. Therefore, you me," she said.

"Oh no, I can't allow you to do that," he

"Please, Hunter, I insist. It's the leas thank a member of law enforcement all safe. Now, what can I get for you t

Although he didn't like the idea his lunch, he also didn't want to ar take one of Big Ed's big burgers wi on the side."

"And what about to drink?"

"A cup of coffee," he replie night ahead of me, because o sick and I'm picking up his

"That's good of you," s sparkled with such bright the crystal clear depths.

a charming grin. "What can I say? It's another normal day at Big Ed's."

"Have you always worked as a waitress?"

"I was a stay-at-home mother until my divorce, and then I went to work waitressing because I knew how to hustle for tips and I could pretty much pick my schedule."

"Are you telling me after all this time you've just been hustling me for tips?" he teased.

She raised a hand up to her lips as if she'd just let a big secret escape. "Oh, I wasn't supposed to tell you that part."

He laughed and then held her gaze for a long moment. "Have I told you today that I find you really attractive?"

"Hush, you're making me blush," she replied. Sure enough, that pink hue leaped into her cheeks.

"I find your blushes utterly charming."

"Ainsley?" Big Ed's voice boomed from the pass-through window.

"Maybe that's your order up." She whirled away from the table and headed to the back.

She returned a moment later with his burger and a deeper blush on her cheeks. "I picked up your order, along with a bit of a scolding."

"Scolding?"

Her gaze didn't quite meet his. "Big Ed said we can flirt with each other a little less and I need to work a little more because I have other patrons to attend to."

"So basically what he's saying is we have to flirt faster," Hunter replied with a grin.

She laughed. "And on that note, I'm leaving your table now."

He watched her scurry away to another table and enjoyed the slight sway of her hips. He looked over at Big Ed, who grinned at him and then shook his head.

Sure to her word, she didn't give him a check when he finished eating, so he tipped her not only the cost of the meal, but also his usual twenty-five percent.

When he left the café, he was even more excited for their next date. He had a feeling that Ainsley Meadows just might be the right woman to help heal the pain of his past.

Bingo.

Peter Waverly closed his computer down and leaned back in his chair in his spacious home office in Portland, Maine. Success…it tasted even better than the thousand-dollar bottle of wine he'd opened to celebrate.

It was true that money could buy you almost anything, and he'd thrown a ton of money out on the dark web to find the answers he'd needed.

A big help in achieving what he needed was the fact that his father had passed away eighteen months before. Jeffrey Waverly had been a very successful businessman worth millions, and upon his death Peter had become a very wealthy man.

Peter now took another sip of his wine and then rose

from his desk. He walked down the hallway to the master bathroom and stared into the mirror over the sink.

A stranger stared back at him. Gone was the blond hair, replaced with a dark brown color. That had been only the beginning of his transformation.

In the last year and a half he'd had a nose job, cheek and chin work done, and implants to fix two crooked front teeth. If his parents were alive right now, they wouldn't recognize him...and neither would *she*.

She wouldn't see him coming. Tomorrow he would begin arrangements to arrive in Dusty Gulch, Kansas. It was past time he have a reunion with his ex-wife, Colette.

He had to teach her a lesson for leaving him. He had to teach her an even bigger lesson for taking his daughter away from him.

He grinned at the man in the mirror. Thoughts of Colette rushed through his head...the intense love he'd felt for her, the all-consuming passion and utter need of her. She had been his entire world, and when she'd given him his daughter, he'd been over the moon with happiness.

Sure, there had been times he'd needed to discipline Colette because she broke one of his rules, but he always told her exactly why she was being disciplined.

And then she'd left him.

The last night they had been together, he'd admit, he lost it. She had made him so angry he'd almost killed her then. Luckily, he had friends in high places, and he'd managed to escape an attempted murder charge.

He'd assumed he and Colette would pick up where they'd left off, but while he'd been locked up for a day, she had run.

He balled up his fist as a white-hot rage gripped him. He slammed his fist into the mirror, shattering it into a million pieces.

That's what he was going to do to Colette. First he intended to break her...and then he was going to kill her.

Chapter Three

"What is this? Date number three?" Juanita's dark eyes twinkled.

"Officially it's date number three, but I kind of feel like we're been on one extended long date," Ainsley replied. "When he comes in for lunch every day, it's like we're having mini-dates."

Once again Juanita was keeping Melinda for the evening so Ainsley could go out with Hunter. The two women were seated at Juanita's kitchen table, and the sound of children's laughter drifted in from the living room.

"You like him." It wasn't a question, it was a statement of fact.

"Oh, Juanita, I do," Ainsley confessed. "Tonight he's grilling steak for me at his house."

"If you've already eaten Chinese and pizza together, other than the café you've hit all the hot eating spots in town," Juanita said with a laugh.

"That's what Hunter told me."

The sparkle in her eyes and her smile dimmed

somewhat as Juanita reached across the table and covered one of Ainsley's hands with hers.

"Try not to break his heart, Ainsley. He's had enough heartache in his life for any one man to carry. Hunter is a good man who deserves much better than what he's been dealt in his past." Juanita pulled her hand back.

"I know he's divorced and that must have been painful for him, but is there more?" Ainsley asked curiously. Hunter hadn't appeared scarred or badly hurt when he'd mentioned his divorce to her.

"There's more, but it's Hunter's story to tell when he's ready. And now, you'd better get out of here or you'll be late for your date with him."

Ainsley nodded and stood. "I feel like I should be paying you for babysitting for me," she said as she walked toward the back door.

"Nonsense, I've told you one more in this household is no big deal. Besides, Melinda is really good with helping with the younger ones. I should probably be paying her for all her help."

Minutes later as Ainsley drove home to get ready for her date, thoughts of her mother and her sister filled her mind, and a deep ache swept over her. Ainsley's father had passed away over ten years ago. Thankfully, he hadn't lived to know the brutality his daughter had gone through.

However, her mother and sister were very much alive, and she missed them terribly. When Ainsley had first gone on the run, she'd made the mistake of believing herself safe and she'd called her mother. It had almost been a deadly error, for the phone call had been traced and he'd nearly found her.

At that time she'd realized she had to function as if her mother and her sister were dead. This had been and continued to be absolutely heartbreaking, but Ainsley was determined to protect not only herself, but more importantly her daughter.

By the time she got back to her apartment, her thoughts were consumed by the man who would pick her up in thirty minutes. There was no question that she was quite smitten with Hunter.

Their last date had gone as well as their first. At the end of that date, he'd once again given her a short, sweet kiss. Her desire to get a real, deep kiss from him was growing by the minute.

As she put on her makeup, she thought about what Juanita had said about Hunter. She'd already believed she'd seen a core of sadness inside Hunter's eyes, and now Juanita's words intrigued her even more.

Try not to break his heart. Juanita's words echoed in her head. That was the last thing Ainsley wanted to do. But she didn't know what the future might hold. She knew Hunter liked her, as she liked him. Should she just stop seeing him to make sure she didn't hurt him? Maybe he would be the one to hurt her.

She was hoping to just let things develop naturally between them. The only way she could see that she might break his heart was if she had to pick up and leave town in the blink of an eye. And she was hoping that wouldn't happen.

She finished getting ready, and by the time she stood in the living room to await Hunter's arrival, all other thoughts of anything else had vanished beneath a rush of sweet anticipation.

Promptly at five o'clock, the knock fell on her door. She grabbed her purse and then opened the door. As always her breath hitched at the sight of him.

"Hi," he said, his eyes sparkling.

"Hi back," she replied.

He grinned. "Ready to go?"

"Ready." She closed the door behind her, and together they walked to his truck.

"Hungry?" he asked once they were on their way.

"I can't wait to see if you can really grill a mean steak as you promised me yesterday at lunch."

"The pressure is definitely on. I'm also baking potatoes and making a salad."

"Sounds like a perfect meal to me." As always the scent of his fresh cologne mingling with a faint hint of minty soap and shaving cream half seduced her.

Within minutes they pulled into the driveway of an attractive beige ranch house with chocolate-brown trim. The lawn was neatly manicured, and a large maple tree stood in the center, sporting the beautiful red leaves of autumn.

"This is lovely," she said as they walked to the front door. "How long have you lived here?"

"About eight years."

"You must have been a baby when you bought it," she replied.

He laughed. "I was young." He unlocked the door and turned to her. "You told me yesterday at lunch that you liked dogs. I have to warn you, when I open this door, we will be met by a small bundle of fur who will threaten to lick you to death."

She playfully straightened her shoulders. "I think I'm ready."

He opened the door, and they stepped inside. Sure enough, a little black dog flew past Hunter and instead began to dance at Ainsley's feet.

"Oh my gosh, aren't you the sweetest thing." Ainsley leaned over, and Zeus jumped into her arms. Zeus kissed her neck as if he was thrilled to see her.

"Uh-oh, you just made a big mistake."

"What's that?" she asked, giggling as Zeus continued to kiss her.

"You picked him up and made nice with him. Now you'll be his slave."

She laughed and put the dog back on the floor. As Zeus finally greeted Hunter, she looked around at her surroundings. The living room was a nice size. The black recliner chair and overstuffed gray sofa suggested this was a room for comfort.

A large television hung on the wall above a gray stone fireplace, and a nearby bookshelf held not only a variety of books but also a framed photo of all the men and women who worked together for the sheriff, and one picture of Hunter with the sheriff and Jake Albright.

"You know the Albrights?" she asked. She had heard about the wealthy, powerful family who owned most of the town. She also knew there had been a huge scandal when Jake Albright's brother had tried to kill Eva Martin, the woman Jake loved and had since married.

"Not well. You heard about his brother and the whole mess?"

She smiled at him and nodded. "Gossip is not in short supply around Dusty Gulch."

"That was definitely a gossip-worthy crime. Anyway, when the dust finally settled, Jake donated money for body cams and for updating other ancient equipment in the department."

"That was nice of him."

"He seems like a real nice guy."

"Are you going to give me the full tour of the house?" She was interested in seeing all the rooms, especially his bedroom.

"Sure," he replied. "Just follow me." He led her down the hallway and gestured into the first door on the left, which was a bathroom done in navy blue.

"Nice," she said.

He grinned. "I'm not much of a decorator, so everything is pretty basic."

"There's nothing wrong with basic."

He smiled at her. "That's one more thing I like about you. No judgment." He opened a door on his right.

"This bedroom I'm using as a home office." There was a desk with a computer and a small bookcase with stacked paperwork.

He gestured to the closed door on the right. "That's just an empty room."

She thought she detected some sudden emotion in his voice, but before she could really process it, he opened the door to the master bedroom.

A king-size bed was covered with a spread in light and dark grays. Two nightstands flanked the bed, each holding attractive lamps. Several black-and-white pictures of landscapes hung on the wall. There was a doorway that led to an adjoining bath.

He gestured toward the bed. "This is where I dream about you."

"Don't you know it's against the law to try to seduce a woman before you feed her?"

He laughed. "I have to confess, that's a law I'm unfamiliar with, but I hope you let me off with just a warning. Maybe it's time I take you to the kitchen before I break that law again."

She followed him back through the living room and into a large airy kitchen with gold-speckled black granite countertops and a center island. The dining table was smoked glass, giving the whole room a sleek, contemporary look. "Please, sit down." He gestured her toward the table.

There were glass sliding doors that led onto a deck. He opened the door, and Zeus ran outside.

"This is really nice, Hunter."

He grinned. "You say that like you thought I might live in a cave."

She laughed in protest. "I definitely didn't mean it that way."

He opened the refrigerator and pulled out a bottle of red wine. "How about a glass?"

"I'd love it."

"Or, if you prefer, I have beer."

"A glass of wine is good."

He pulled a bottle of beer from the fridge. "I'm more of a beer kind of guy."

"Is there anything I can do to help with dinner?"

"No. Just sit tight and relax." He poured the wine and set the long-stem glass in front of her. "I've got the potatoes baking and the salad chilling. All I have to do is put the steaks on the grill."

He joined her at the table. "Did I mention how lovely you look tonight?"

"No, you didn't, and thank you." She'd worn jeans with a lightweight lavender sweater that she knew somehow accentuated the blue of her eyes.

"I didn't really get much of a chance to talk to you when you came into the café yesterday. So, how was your day? Anything exciting happen?" she asked.

"The most exciting thing today was trying to tell Madge Renfro that it wasn't an emergency calling for excessive speeding to get her dog Pookie to her grooming appointment. She was going fifty-eight in a thirty-mile-an-hour speed zone. She then proceeded to tell me that Pookie had poopie on her bottom and needed the groomer to clean her up, because it was stinky and Madge doesn't do stinky." He grinned and shook his head ruefully. "The life of a small-town cop…"

Ainsley laughed. "Did you give her a speeding ticket?"

"No, I wound up giving her a stern warning."

"Ah, so at heart you're just a softie," she replied teasingly.

"Don't mistake my compassion as weakness." His eyes glittered with a look of determination and strength. "If anyone comes after me or the people I care about, they will be met with a force they've never seen before. And now I think it's time I get the steaks on."

He was the kind of man she'd once dreamed of being with…strong and confident. He made her feel safe and protected, but nobody could protect her from her ex-husband. She could only hope she was truly safe in this small town and that the two men would never, ever meet.

SHE WAS EVERYTHING he'd hoped to find. Hunter was definitely crazy about Ainsley. As they ate dinner, he told her about some of the funny things he'd encountered in his work.

He loved the sound of her laughter and the way her eyes sparkled with mirth. He found himself reaching for stories that would make her laugh again and again.

She, in turn, shared with him funny things that happened in the café. He was thrilled that their humor was very similar. It was important in a relationship to be able to laugh together.

Their conversation grew more serious as they spoke about their parents. "Mine moved to a senior living place in Kansas City two years ago," he said. "I try to drive out and see them about once a month or so."

"That's nice. Unfortunately my parents passed away in a car accident five years ago."

"Do you have siblings?" he asked.

She shook her head and stared down at her plate. "No, I'm an only child." She gazed back up at him. "What about you? Do you have brothers or sisters?"

"Nope, like you I'm an only child."

"When I was younger I made up a sister. Her name was Lily, and she was a year older than me. She played with me, and as I got a little older she gave me fashion advice and we would talk and giggle long into the night."

He smiled. "You definitely talk about her like she was real."

Once again she looked down at her plate. "She was definitely real to me for a little while." She looked back up at him, and there was a touch of embarrassment in her eyes. "You probably think I'm crazy."

"Not at all," he assured her. "You sound like you must have been a lonely child."

She shrugged. "That was then and this is now."

They finished the meal, and he insisted she remain seated as he cleaned up the dishes. Then he poured her a fresh glass of wine and he grabbed another beer.

He let Zeus back inside, and they went into the living room.

Zeus jumped up on the recliner and looked at Hunter expectantly. However, for tonight Zeus was out of luck. Hunter would much rather sit on the sofa next to Ainsley.

He sat close to her, smelling the heady scent of her and feeling her body heat warming him. For the last three weeks, a tremendous desire for her had been building inside him.

He desperately wanted to pull her into his arms and feel her body against his. He wanted to kiss her lush lips until they were both breathless. But he didn't do any of that.

Their conversation was light and easy. Zeus finally gave up, jumped down from the recliner and curled up in his bed next to the fireplace.

"Tell me about your daughter," he said when the conversation between them momentarily stalled.

Her face lit up with a beautiful smile. "She's the absolute best thing that ever happened to me. She's smart and funny and has the sweetest heart in the whole wide world. Of course I might be just a wee bit prejudiced."

"Mothers are supposed to believe their children are all that and a bag of chips," he replied with a smile. "Because she's your daughter, I believe she's smart and funny and has a sweet heart. I would also believe that she's beautiful like you."

Her cheeks dusted with color. "Why, Deputy

Churchill, you sweet-talk me like that and I'll think you're trying to seduce me again."

"Maybe that's exactly what I'm trying to do." His heart suddenly raced as he held her gaze. There was a stillness about her. Her tongue slid out as if to dampen overdry lips, and then those moist lips opened slightly and she raised her face to his.

Even though he saw open invitation in her mouth, in her eyes, he still wanted to make sure. "May I kiss you, Ainsley?"

"Please," she replied.

He leaned forward and placed his lips on hers. Heat swept through him and his heart raced faster, especially as she raised her arms and wound them around his neck.

He pulled her even closer to him and deepened the kiss by swirling his tongue with hers. This kiss was everything and more than he'd imagined it would be.

It was a confirmation that this was a woman he wanted more from, not only physically but also emotionally. He was all in to see where this relationship would go, and he was hoping it would go the distance.

The kiss continued for several long moments, and then he softly kissed across her jawline and down her throat. She clutched at his shoulders as if afraid he'd stop, and that only shot his desire for her even higher.

She was close enough to him now that he could feel the press of her full breasts against his chest. He wanted her…he wanted to pick her up and carry her into his bedroom. He wanted to feel her naked body next to his.

He captured her lips once again with his, and when the kiss ended she unwound her arms from around his neck and leaned back from him.

"You're a dangerous man, Deputy Churchill," she said half breathlessly.

"And you're a dangerous woman," he replied. He reached out and touched a length of her long, black hair. "I have to confess, Ainsley, I have a lot of desire for you."

"And I have a lot for you." Her eyes glistened as she held his gaze. "But I...we need to take things slowly."

"I can do that. Whatever you need from me, Ainsley. You're in charge of our physical relationship. You tell me if and when you're ready."

"Thank you. I appreciate you understanding."

"Is it too soon to ask to meet your daughter?" he asked. "Or am I rushing things?"

A small frown danced across her forehead. It smoothed out and she smiled. "How about next Thursday you come to my place for dinner and then you two can meet."

"That sounds great." He knew her agreement was a deepening of their relationship. He felt as if finally fate was casting down a light of positivity on his life, and he was excited about what the future would bring.

"Unfortunately, it's time for me to get home," she said and stood from the sofa.

Reluctantly Hunter stood as well. "Just let me grab my keys and gun, and I'll get you home."

Minutes later they walked out of the house together. "It's a beautiful night," she said.

He was about to answer her when movement next to his porch snagged his attention. Immediately he saw a man hiding in his bushes. He grabbed his gun and pushed Ainsley behind him. "Who's there? Step out where I can see you with your hands up."

Adrenaline pumped through him as he held his gun steady, ready for anything that might happen next. While he knew many of the townspeople liked and respected him, he also knew there were some who took offense when they or their loved ones were arrested.

"I said, come out of those bushes with your hands up," he commanded again.

The shadowed figure moved out of the bushes, and Hunter swore and lowered his gun. "Jeez, George, you were just about to get yourself shot. What are you doing skulking around out here?"

"I didn't mean no harm," George replied. He held out a package of cookies. "I just wanted to give these to you to thank you for taking care of me when Marybeth was gone. Then you stepped out here with your lady friend and I thought maybe the time wasn't right."

"Next time make yourself known and don't hide in the bushes." Hunter holstered his gun. He then took the package of cookies from him and introduced him to Ainsley.

"You didn't have to bring me cookies, George," he said.

"I just wanted you to know that I'm mighty thankful for your friendship." He offered a shy smile to Ainsley. "He's a mighty good man, Miss Ainsley, and now I'll just leave you two to carry on."

As they got into Hunter's vehicle, George meandered down the sidewalk back to his house. "That was sweet of him," Ainsley said.

"He's a nice guy. He's just got some issues," Hunter replied.

"Must be kind of strange to work law enforcement in a town where everyone knows where you live," she said.

"It has its moments. I occasionally get my vehicle egged, but most of the time people respect my privacy, and I haven't had any real trouble."

"That's good."

They small-talked on the rest of the way to her apartment, and then it was time to tell her good-night. "Thank you, Hunter, for another wonderful night."

"I really look forward to Thursday nights when I get to spend time with you."

She smiled up at him. "Me too." She leaned toward him, and he gathered her into his arms.

"Is it too soon to tell you that I see a bright future ahead of us?" he asked.

Her eyes darkened and seemed to shutter closed against him. It lasted only a moment, and then she gave him one of her beautiful smiles. "I feel the same way. And now it's time for a good-night kiss."

"With pleasure." This time he kissed her softly and then stepped back from her. "I'll see you tomorrow for lunch."

"I'll be here."

Minutes later as Hunter drove back home, he thought about that moment when her eyes had darkened as if hiding secrets. Had he only imagined it? Had it somehow been a trick of the night shadows?

He hoped so, because the last woman he'd been involved with had had a ton of devastating secrets, and he never wanted to engage with a woman like that again.

Chapter Four

Ainsley sank down on the edge of Melinda's bed. "Did you have fun tonight with Bonnie?" She swept a strand of her daughter's honey-colored hair away from Melinda's beautiful blue eyes.

"We had lots of fun. We played pretend and I was the queen and Bonnie was a princess. We decided to make Henry the king and we colored him a crown, but he tried to eat it."

Ainsley laughed. Henry was eighteen months old, the youngest of Juanita's children. She leaned forward and kissed Melinda on her cheek. "Have sweet dreams, my little angel."

"I will," Melinda replied. Ainsley started to get up. "Mom, last night Daddy talked to me."

Ainsley's breath caught in her chest. "Melinda, honey, you know Daddy can't talk to you. I told you, Daddy went away and he's never coming back."

"But he told me last night that he *was* coming back for me because he loved me more than anything else in the whole wide world." Melinda looked at her earnestly.

"You must have had a dream," Ainsley said.

"It wasn't a dream. I wasn't even asleep when he talked to me," she replied.

"You tell me if he talks to you again, okay?" Ainsley stood. "Now you need to go to sleep. It's getting late and you have school tomorrow."

"Okay, good night." Melinda turned over and closed her eyes, and Ainsley left the small bedroom.

It was only when Ainsley was in her own bed that she allowed herself to think of what Melinda had said. It had been at least a year since Melinda had even mentioned her father.

At that time Ainsley had seriously considered telling the little girl that her father was dead, but ultimately she hadn't done that. Instead she'd told Melinda that her father had been sent far, far away and would never be able to see them again.

There was no question in her mind that either Melinda had dreamed of her father talking to her or it had been the fantasy of a little girl who didn't have her father around.

Still, the mention of her ex-husband stirred all kinds of memories in Ainsley, horrible memories that transferred into nightmares that plagued her for what felt like the entire night.

She awakened late the next morning. She threw herself together, checked on Melinda and then raced into the café to get things going for the day.

By the time Lana came in so that Ainsley could go back and get Melinda up and ready for school, Ainsley was still flustered and off-kilter because of the nightmares that had chased her through the night.

"Girl, sit down and I'll pour you a cup of coffee. You need to calm down before the breakfast rush really starts," Lana said. "You're as shaky as my third husband wearing a pair of my high heels."

Ainsley laughed. "I'm not sure I want to hear that whole story."

Lana pointed to the end stool at the counter. "Sit." The gray-haired woman poured Ainsley a cup of coffee. "What's going on with you this morning?"

"Nothing really. I had nightmares all night and then overslept this morning, and I've just been off since then."

"I hate nightmares. One of my worst nightmares involves my second husband, a plucked pink chicken and a horse wearing a big straw hat."

Ainsley couldn't help but laugh, which she knew was exactly what Lana had wanted. "You're the best, Lana."

Lana grinned and then her smile faded. "So, what were your nightmares about?"

"The boogeyman chasing me through the shadows."

"Ah, boogeyman dreams are the worst. Sit and drink your coffee. I've got the diners in here right now."

Lana got up as Big Ed yelled, "Order up!"

Ainsley sat for only a minute or two and then she

slid off the stool. The breakfast rush would begin in earnest in the next fifteen minutes or so.

She released a deep sigh when Richard Adams walked in and sat at one of her tables. Ainsley guessed Richard to be in his midsixties. He was a big, burly man and more than a bit of a curmudgeon. He was also a crummy tipper—if he tipped at all, it was usually a single dollar.

"Good morning, Richard." She greeted him with a smile.

"What's good about it?" He scowled at her.

"The sun is shining and good food is cooking, so I'd say that's a great start to the day. Now, what can I get for you?"

"I'll take the breakfast special, but I want some cheese in the scrambled eggs and extra onions in the hash browns. I want the bacon extra crispy and the toast light. I'll also have a cup of coffee and a glass of orange juice. Think you can get all that right?"

"I'll do my very best," Ainsley replied. She placed the order and then hurried to get his coffee and juice. "Here we go," she said as she served his drinks.

"I hope the coffee is fresh. Last time you served me, the coffee tasted burned and nasty."

Ainsley suppressed a sigh and kept her smile in place. "This coffee was brewed fifteen minutes ago, so it should be nice and fresh for you."

She had no idea why Richard always chose to sit in her section when he obviously didn't like her. She smiled as she approached the table next to Richard, where Jimmy Miller sat.

Jimmy was a young, friendly man who worked as a ranch hand for Eva and Jake Albright. "Hey, Jimmy. We don't usually see you here in the mornings," she said.

"Jake gave me the morning off, so I decided to come in here and see you." His blue eyes twinkled. "I can't think of a better way to start my morning than to see your pretty face."

Ainsley laughed. "Have you ever considered bottling that charm?"

"It's just too good to be bottled." Jimmy's smile faltered. "But I guess it's not enough to win you away from Hunter Churchill. He's got a badge and a gun… kind of hard to compete with a man like that."

"Let's talk about food, Jimmy. What can I get you this morning?" she asked, hoping to get off the personal turn of the conversation.

An hour later the dining room was almost empty as the breakfast crowd left and the lunch group had yet to show up.

"I hope you didn't let that turd Richard get under your skin," Lana said as the two stood next to the soda machine.

"I have to admit, it's hard not to take his complaints personally," Ainsley admitted. "He acts like I never do anything right."

"At least you had that young buck Jimmy making goo-goo eyes at you."

Ainsley laughed. "Jimmy seems like a nice guy, but…"

"But it's that fine Deputy Churchill who floats your boat."

"Hey, ladies, why don't you come back here and we can have a tea party together and socialize all you want," Ed said sarcastically.

"Don't get your underwear twisted," Lana yelled back. "You know we're the best darned waitresses in town."

The two women parted ways at the coffee machine and readied the tables for the lunch rush. Immediately anticipation started working inside Ainsley. She knew once the lunch rush was over, Hunter would be in.

A thrill swept through her as she thought of the kisses they had shared the night before. There had been a part of her that had wanted to throw caution to the wind and make love with him. But when they did make love, she didn't want to have to rush because she had to leave to get Melinda by a certain time.

She was excited about taking the next step with him, and that was introducing him to Melinda. She couldn't imagine her daughter not liking Hunter. And she certainly hoped that Hunter would love her daughter.

For the first time in what felt like years, there was real hope in Ainsley's heart. Sure, eventually she'd have to tell him about the lies she'd told him. But she hadn't lied to him about anything except a couple of factual things.

She'd been truthful with him about everything that

formed the very core of her. She'd shared deep feelings with him about a number of things that shared her code of ethics, her sense of morality and the kind of woman she really was. Besides, hopefully by the time she decided to tell him the truth, he'd be so madly in love with her it wouldn't matter.

Is it safe?

For the first time since she'd run from the home she'd shared with her abusive husband, she believed the answer was yes. It was finally safe for her to pursue life to its fullest.

And she desperately wanted to do that with Hunter.

TONIGHT MARKED A month of Hunter and Ainsley officially dating. As he dressed for the date, adrenaline rushed through him as he anticipated spending more quality time with her.

He'd bought a stuffed pink unicorn for Melinda and a bouquet of a variety of flowers for Ainsley. The bouquet was bright and colorful and reminded him of Ainsley's playful, beautiful spirit.

He knew that tonight was the most important date he'd have with Ainsley. It was so vital that Melinda liked him. He knew that if the little girl didn't like him then the odds of the relationship further deepening were probably nil.

Nerves jangled through him as he drove to her place. He was interested to see the apartment she called home. He'd never been inside the living quarters at the back of the café, and his interest was piqued.

There was no question in his mind that he was falling in love with Ainsley. All the barriers he'd had up after his ex-wife's betrayals had been tumbling down since the first date he'd had with Ainsley.

He was ready to trust again. He was ready to love again, and the place he found himself in both mentally and emotionally excited him.

By the time he pulled up behind the café, his nerves had calmed and he just felt the sweet anticipation of seeing her once again.

He got out with the flowers and stuffed unicorn in hand. He was about to knock on the door when it opened and Ainsley greeted him with a smile. "Punctual as always."

"I always try to be on time." He thrust the flowers toward her. "These are for you, and the unicorn is for Melinda."

"Ah, do you always bribe the women in your life with gifts?" She took the flowers from him with a teasing glint in her eyes.

"Not always, but sometimes."

"Come on in." She opened the door wider to allow him inside. "Melinda is in her room. I'll call her out in a few minutes."

"Hmm, something smells really good," he said as he stepped into a small living room.

"Homemade enchiladas with cheesy refried beans and rice on the side. Come on into the kitchen."

The living room held a navy sofa, where he placed the unicorn, a coffee table and an entertainment center that held a small television. The kitchen was small as well, a square wooden table shoved against one wall taking up most of the room. She motioned him into one of the three chairs. The table was already set with navy blue plates and silverware.

"This is called intimate living. I can almost sit at the table and stir something on my stove at the same time," she said with a laugh.

"I find it quite nice," he replied. He watched as she placed the flowers on the counter and then reached into a bottom cabinet and retrieved a vase.

"You're very nice," she replied with a sweet smile. "This place is just a resting place. I'm hoping eventually to rent a house or at least get into a bigger apartment. While I really appreciate Big Ed for letting us stay here, I don't want Melinda to grow up in this tiny apartment."

While she was talking she arranged the flowers and then set them on the table. "There, a nice bright note to the room," she said and then moved to the oven, opened the door and then closed it again. "This should all be ready in the next fifteen minutes or so."

"Is there anything I can do?" he asked.

"Just sit. How about a beer?" She opened the fridge and brought out the brand of beer that he drank.

"I wouldn't turn my nose up at that," he replied.

For the next few minutes, they caught up on their days as she stirred the contents in two saucepans on the stovetop. Despite the odors of Mexican spices that filled the air, he could still smell the floral fragrance of her perfume. It was a scent he found incredibly sexy.

She was clad in a pair of black jeans and a fitted royal blue blouse that did amazing things to her eyes. Yes, he was definitely on the verge of falling helplessly and hopelessly in love with her.

She took another peek into the oven and then pronounced the meal ready to serve. "Why don't you come with me to get Melinda? That way you can give her the unicorn."

"That sounds good to me." He was eager to meet her daughter, who would surely become an important part of his life and heart in the future.

As he followed her back through the living room, he picked up the unicorn from the sofa. There were three doorways, one that led to the bathroom, one that apparently was Ainsley's bedroom and the third room where her daughter slept and played.

He would have liked to get a glimpse of the bedroom where Ainsley slept. He wanted to know the color of her bedspread so he could imagine himself beneath it with her.

"Melinda, our guest is here, and he has a surprise for you," Ainsley said.

"A surprise for me?" Melinda stepped into her doorway. She was a petite girl with blond hair and her mother's beautiful blue eyes.

"Hi, Melinda. My name is Hunter." He held out the unicorn. "This is for you. It doesn't have a name yet. I thought you might want to give it a name."

Melinda took the unicorn from him, but her eyes held more than a bit of distrust. She looked at her mother and then back at him. "Thank you."

"Why don't you put the unicorn on the sofa and you can think about a name while we eat dinner," Ainsley said.

They left the small hallway and headed back to the kitchen. Melinda sat in the chair opposite him, and Ainsley opened the oven and pulled out a large baking dish and set it in the center of the table.

"There's both meat and cheese enchiladas," she said as she spooned beans into a serving bowl and then did the same with the rice.

"Do you like Mexican food, Melinda?" The girl hadn't made eye contact with him since they'd sat down.

"I like pizza better," she said, not taking her gaze off the plate in front of her.

"Pizza is also a favorite of mine," he replied. "What kind do you like? I like pepperoni."

"Just cheese. I like cheese pizza," she replied.

The rest of the meal made it to the table, and then Ainsley sat. "Dig in," she said.

"How about I serve you two," he said and picked up Melinda's plate. "What would you like? Meat or cheese?"

"Cheese," she replied.

Hunter ladled out a cheese enchilada on the plate. "Would you like some beans and rice?"

"Some beans."

Hunter fixed the plate and then slid it in front of her. "What about you, Ainsley?"

"I can serve myself. You go ahead and fill your plate," she replied.

He took one meat, one cheese and a helping of the side dishes. Once Ainsley had served herself, they all began to eat. "This is delicious," he said after a few bites. "Does your mother always cook this good?" he asked Melinda.

She shrugged. "Mostly we eat in the café."

"And mostly that's true," Ainsley said. "Most nights I'm so tired from working all day, and the café makes it easy for us to have dinner there."

He hated that she had to work so hard, that when she worked she had very long hours. If they married, he'd make sure she would waitress only if she wanted to.

As they ate he tried to engage with Melinda, but she was having nothing to do with him. Each time the girl answered him in monosyllables and with no eye contact, the frown on Ainsley's forehead increased.

They finished the meal and Melinda jumped up from the table. "Can I go back to my room now?" she asked.

"Before you go, did you come up with a name for the unicorn?" Hunter asked.

"I'm going to name her Ella." For the first time Melinda made eye contact with him. "Just because you bought her for me doesn't mean I have to like you."

"Melinda," Ainsley said in obvious surprise.

"Well, it's true. Daddy said I shouldn't like him because Daddy is coming to get me and Mr. Hunter just wants to get into your pants."

Hunter wasn't sure who gasped louder, him or Ainsley. "Melinda Marie, march yourself into your bedroom right now."

"I'm just saying what Daddy told me to say," Melinda protested as her eyes began to glaze with tears.

"Go." Ainsley pointed to the bedroom.

Melinda released a little sob and then raced to her room and slammed the door behind her. Ainsley turned to look at him, her cheeks pink. "I'm so sorry...I don't know what's going on with her."

"If you need to speak to her, I can cool my heels right here."

She looked at him with relief. "I'll be right back."

He watched as she hurried to her daughter's bedroom. Wow, there was no question he'd been shocked by what the little girl had said. It made him wonder where she had heard the adult, rather nasty words.

He hadn't expected it to be love at first sight with Melinda, but he certainly hadn't expected this. Ainsley was gone about fifteen minutes, and then she came back into the kitchen.

She sank down in her chair and shook her head. "I'm worried about her. She insists that my ex-husband talks to her at night, but of course that's impossible. For the last couple of years, after the divorce, she didn't really mention my ex-husband, even though she'd thought of herself as a daddy's girl at one time. I don't know if she's just imagining or dreaming about him or if she's having some sort of strange psychological issues that include auditory hallucinations."

"I'm not sure if this helps, but there is a psychologist in town who works with adults and children. Her name is June Atkins. She used to practice in Kansas City and moved out here to retire, but she is still taking patients here in town."

Hunter knew June because for a couple of months after his child had died and his wife had left him, he'd had sessions with the psychologist to help him climb out of his depression.

"Can you give me her information?" she asked.

"I'll text it to you, and now I'll help you clear the dishes."

"Oh no, you don't. You're my guest, and that means you get to just sit while I do the cleanup. Besides, it won't take me long at all." She got up and began to clear the table.

"The meal was really delicious," he said.

"Thanks. Mexican food is one of my very favorites. Too bad we don't have a Mexican restaurant in town."

He laughed. "As small as this town is, I'd say we're lucky to have the café, the Chinese restaurant and a pizza place, plus a couple of drive-through hamburger joints."

"I suppose you're right. The town isn't big enough to have cuisine from all around the world." She grew quiet as she continued to work to put the dinner leftovers away.

He knew she was probably still worried about her

daughter, and as much as he would like to spend the rest of the evening with her, he believed at this point she'd rather be alone.

"Why don't we go back into the living room?" she suggested once the kitchen was completely cleaned up.

"Why don't I get out of here?" He stood and walked over to her. He gently stroked down the side of her face with two fingers. "I really don't think you're in the mood to entertain tonight."

She sighed, but she didn't object. Instead she captured his hand with hers and squeezed tight. "Thank you, Hunter."

They walked to the front door. "I'll text you Dr. Atkins's information as soon as I get home."

She nodded, and he bent down and kissed her on the cheek. She leaned against him for a long moment and then straightened. "Let me know if I can help in any way," he said.

"You're helping right now." She smiled up at him, but the smile wasn't as bright as usual. "I'll see you tomorrow for lunch."

"I wouldn't miss it," he replied. He stepped out of the apartment and into the night air.

Worry rode with him back to his house, the worry that his relationship with Ainsley was now threatened by a pint-size little girl who apparently had no intention of allowing him into her life.

Chapter Five

Ainsley pulled up in front of a two-story house just off Main Street. Her heart beat with anxiety as she parked and then turned off the car engine.

"I don't know why you just don't believe me," Melinda said from the back seat. "I don't want to talk to anyone who is going to try to make me believe I'm just dreaming when Daddy talks to me at night."

"I'm sure that's not what Dr. Atkins is going to try to do," Ainsley replied, although she really had no idea how Dr. Atkins was going to try to help Melinda. All she knew was something needed to be done.

It was late Wednesday afternoon, and Ainsley had taken off work to bring Melinda here. Since the disrupted date with Hunter the Thursday before, Melinda had continued to talk about her daddy coming to get her soon and how he spoke to her at night. She was also becoming more and more disrespectful to Ainsley, per Daddy's instructions.

"It's time for us to go in and meet Dr. Atkins," she now said and opened her car door.

"I still think this is dumb," Melinda grumbled as she got out of the car.

Maybe it was dumb, but Ainsley was desperate to get somebody else's opinion about what was going on with Melinda. June Atkins had been very nice on the phone when Ainsley had called her and explained what had been happening with her daughter. When Ainsley had made the appointment, she was instructed to walk around to the back of the house, where apparently the garage had been converted into an office.

Ainsley knocked on the door, and June Atkins answered. She appeared to be in her late sixties or early seventies. Her hair was a beautiful silver and she had kind blue eyes.

She ushered them into a little waiting room painted in pale blue and with a blue flowered love seat. A coffee table held several magazines for both men and women.

"Please, have a seat." She pointed to the love seat, and she sat in a wing-back chair that matched the love seat. She offered them a warm smile. "It's so nice to meet you both. Melinda, I'm especially excited to get to know you better."

Melinda didn't respond.

The smile on Dr. Atkins's face didn't waver. "Mom, why don't you relax out here while I take Melinda into my office for a private chat?"

She stood, and Ainsley prodded her daughter with her elbow to get her up. "I promise I don't bite," Dr. Atkins said.

A small smile crossed Melinda's lips. "I didn't think you would bite me."

The two disappeared behind a door, and Ainsley blew out a deep, weary sigh. It was exhausting to worry about a loved one. Melinda was her very heart and soul, and she didn't know what was happening to turn her sweet, loving child into a stranger.

Had the trigger for Melinda's odd behavior been the knowledge that her mother was now dating? Something that hadn't happened since the two of them had run from Portland? Run from Peter?

If she had to give up Hunter to fix Melinda's mental health, then she would do that. But even thinking about that option made her heart twist with an ache she hadn't thought possible.

In four short weeks, Hunter had already worked his way deep into her heart. She hadn't realized how deep until this moment, when she had to contemplate telling him goodbye.

She'd had such hope that finally she was going to get to live the fairy tale of love with a good man. But there was no way she could sacrifice her daughter for her own happiness.

The minutes ticked by with agonizing slowness. What were they talking about in there? Would Melinda inadvertently say something that would bring a scrutiny to Ainsley's life that she couldn't afford?

Peter had always been good at keeping his abuse of Ainsley under wraps and separate from their daughter. Many nights Ainsley had suffered in silence and lied to her little girl about black eyes and split lips so Melinda wouldn't know the truth about her father.

In any case, Peter hadn't been a hands-on kind of father, and often several days and nights would go by without him even asking about his daughter. Even though he'd been the one who had told Melinda she was a daddy's girl, the truth was the two hadn't been close.

For the past three years Melinda had seemed to accept that their vagabond lifestyle was normal and they were just seeking the perfect place to call their forever home.

She hadn't talked much about Peter, and Ainsley just assumed with the passing of time that Melinda had very few memories of her father and didn't miss him at all.

Until this…these nighttime disturbances that had Melinda believing her father was coming for her. Once again Ainsley released a deep sigh as she stared at the closed office door.

She didn't know how long these sessions lasted, but she did know how much they cost. Unfortunately, health care wasn't in the budget at the moment. That was a whole different worry. She was hoping to at least be able to make enough in the near future to get Melinda some kind of health-care coverage, but that hadn't happened yet. Still, she would work as many shifts as possible, sell whatever little she possessed to see that Melinda got the help she needed.

Finally the door reopened, and the two walked back

out. Both were smiling. "Melinda, can you wait out here for a few minutes so I can talk to your mother?" Dr. Atkins asked.

Ainsley dug her phone out of her purse and handed it to Melinda. "You can play your games while I'm gone." Melinda grabbed the phone and sat on the love seat while Ainsley followed Dr. Atkins into her office.

The inner office held a nice oversize chair with a coffee table next to it and a small desk with a computer on top and a black swivel desk chair.

"Please sit." Dr. Atkins gestured her to the over-stuffed chair. Ainsley sat and leaned forward.

"First of all, you have a charming and very bright daughter," Dr. Atkins said.

"Thank you," Ainsley replied.

"She's also very stubborn in her belief that she talks to her father at night, but I gave her some things to think about and hopefully we can start working to make her see that this is a fantasy."

"So, that's what you believe it is?"

"I believe it's the longing of a little girl who doesn't have her father in her life."

"But why now? Do you think this has something to do with the fact that I'm dating? Should I stop seeing the man?"

"I would not recommend you stop dating. We don't want to give that kind of power to an eight-year-old girl. It's possible it was triggered at school or whatever. What I recommend for now is that you continue to listen to her, but don't engage in a battle with her. I'm hoping I can appeal to her intelligence."

The psychologist smiled. "I don't think this is a long-term issue. I'd like to see her next week at this same time, if that's okay with you."

"That's fine. I feel so much better now that I've spoken to you," Ainsley replied. "We'll definitely be here next week."

She stood as the doctor did the same. "I'm confident we can get this cleared up in just a couple of sessions." She opened the office door, and they stepped out.

Melinda got up from the love seat and handed Ainsley back her phone. "Melinda, it was nice visiting with you," Dr. Atkins said.

"Thank you," the young girl replied.

Minutes later mother and daughter were back in the car and heading home. "Did you like Dr. Atkins?" Ainsley asked.

"She was nice. She didn't believe me about Daddy, but she was still nice," Melinda replied.

"How do you know she didn't believe you?"

"'Cause of the questions she asked me." Melinda frowned. "I don't want to talk about it anymore. Can we stop for ice cream on the way home?"

"I think I can make that happen," Ainsley replied.

The rest of the evening passed peacefully. Even though it was early, once Melinda was in bed Ainsley took a long hot shower, changed into her nightgown and then got into bed.

She held her cell phone in her hand, and after several moments of thinking about it, she punched in Hunter's phone number.

He answered on the first ring. "I was just thinking about you," he said.

His deep voice smoothed all the rough edges inside her. "And what were you thinking?"

"Since I didn't get into the café for lunch today, I was just thinking how much I missed seeing you and wondering if we're going to get together tomorrow night?"

"I'd love to get together tomorrow night," she replied.

"I was afraid you might not want to see me again."

"I was afraid about that, too. But we had our first appointment with Dr. Atkins today, and she assured me that it was okay for us to continue to date despite Melinda's current attitude toward you."

"That's good to hear." There was obvious relief in his voice. "I'm hoping Melinda will warm up to me as time goes on."

"We stopped on the way home to get ice cream, and I told her that no matter what her father said to her at night, she knows the difference between right and wrong and good behavior and bad. I told her I expected her to act appropriately."

"Did she listen to you?"

"I believe she did. Time will tell. So, what are the plans for tomorrow evening?" She cuddled down in the blanket, happy that she was ending the night with a phone call with the man who was quickly winning her heart.

"Whatever we do together, I'll be happy," he said.

"Why don't we go to your house and hang out watching television and eating popcorn," she suggested.

"That sounds good to me," he replied. "But I think I'll order pizza for us to eat before I break out the popcorn."

"How about you let me get the pizza, Hunter?"

"That's not necessary, Ainsley."

"I know it's not necessary, but it isn't always necessary for you to pay every time we get together."

"I'm an old-fashioned kind of guy. I like taking care of the woman I'm dating. I'll let you know if and when it becomes a problem, deal?"

She hesitated a moment. "Deal," she finally replied.

They spoke a few more minutes and then hung up. Ainsley plugged her phone into the charger and then settled in to sleep. She was falling fast for Hunter Churchill. He was everything she'd ever wanted in her life.

She loved his patience and his kind heart. She adored his smile and the sound of his deep, rumbling laughter. She absolutely loved the sound of her name falling from his lips. She just wished it was her real name.

The closer she got to him, the more she worried

about the lies she'd told him. Could she go the rest of her life living the lie? As she drifted to sleep, she had no answer.

PETER HAD BEEN busy since he'd learned the location of his ex-wife. He'd bought himself a farm fifteen minutes from Dusty Gulch. It was a simple three-bedroom house, nothing like what he was accustomed to, but it was completely isolated and perfect for what he had in mind.

He now stood in front of the bank of computer monitors that showed him images of Colette's little apartment. Both Melinda and Colette were asleep, so there would be no more activity happening tonight.

He'd been enjoying having conversations with Melinda after he knew Colette was in her own bedroom at night. It had been particularly fun to watch her misbehave at his command.

Having the cameras and microphones installed there had been fairly easy. All he'd needed was to find somebody who could give him access to the café attic.

He'd found that person in Ted Johnson, the janitor/maintenance man who worked at night at the café. Ted was sixty-three years old and worked hard to earn just a little bit more than minimum wage.

When Peter offered the man ten thousand dollars for two nights of access to the attic and not telling a soul about it, Ted had jumped at the opportunity.

The two nights had allowed Peter to set up the electronics he needed to watch and listen into the tiny two-bedroom apartment where his angel and his bitch of an ex-wife were staying.

He now stretched with his arms overhead and then left the bedroom. He locked the door behind him and then looked into the master bedroom, where Sheila Turrel was sprawled across the bed.

Sheila was the perfect woman he needed for now. He'd gone trolling for somebody just like her at a dive bar in Dusty Gulch called the Wrecking Ball.

The thirty-six-year-old woman was thin as a rail and not pretty, but she was also a heavy drinker and a heroin user, which made her very attractive to him.

As long as he kept her hooked up, she would be the best alibi he could have if for some reason he came under suspicion.

She stayed nodded out most of the time and had no idea when he was home and when he wasn't, but she would swear he'd been with her if anyone from law enforcement asked. Although he found her a weak, disgusting waste of a human being, he needed her right now to assure his own safety.

He continued walking down the hallway and into the kitchen. He flipped on the light against the darkness of night and then opened the back door and stepped out on the back porch.

The smell struck him first. It was an odor of musk and filth, of urine and feces. Grunts and rustling filled the otherwise silent night.

He didn't have to see the pigs to know they were

there. When he'd bought the farm, he'd paid extra for the herd of pigs the farmer owned.

According to what he'd read, there were far too many pigs in the small pen where they were kept and Peter was making sure they all stayed nice and hungry.

The most important thing he'd learned about pigs was that sixteen of them could completely eat a human body in eight minutes. There were currently twenty-five pigs in the pen.

This pen of hungry pigs was perfect for tying up any loose ends. Right now there were two—Ted and Sheila.

Ultimately the pigs were his ex-wife's fate.

Colette had wanted to disappear from his life. Now he was going to make sure she disappeared from life altogether. He drew in the nasty scent of the pigs.

Yes, it all smelled bad...but it also smelled of sweet revenge.

"THE PIZZA SMELLS delicious," Ainsley said as she walked into Hunter's kitchen.

"Half pepperoni and half mushroom and green pepper," he replied as he got out two plates and napkins.

Ainsley sat at the table. She was touched that he had remembered the kind of pizza she liked. It meant he paid attention, and that made her feel very special.

"Beer or soda?" he asked.

"Soda is fine for me."

Within minutes they were both seated at the table and enjoying the pizza. "It was another fairly quiet day for me, which is just the way I like my days," he said between bites.

"My day started with me having to deny service to Ben Wilkins. He came in highly intoxicated. He was loud and belligerent, so I told him he needed to leave," she said.

"Did he comply?" Hunter asked. His green eyes darkened as he held her gaze.

"He screamed and cursed at me, and then Big Ed escorted him out of the building," she replied.

"Big Ed should have called me. You should never have to endure that kind of abuse."

"Down, tiger," she replied with a laugh, although she was secretly thrilled by the protective light that shone from his beautiful eyes.

"I don't like anyone talking disrespectfully to you," he replied.

She laughed once again. "It's a hazard of working in food service."

"Then you should get hazard pay."

She grinned at him. He looked amazingly handsome tonight in a pair of jeans and a forest green shirt that did wonderful things to his eyes.

She'd never dreamed it could be so easy, that a relationship could feel so warm and comfortable. She'd never believed she was worthy of a man like Hunter. He made her feel so many ways she hadn't felt before… witty and funny, smart and beautiful. Whenever she was with him, she felt protected and safe.

She wished she had met him years ago. She wished

she had met him instead of Peter. But then she wouldn't have Melinda, and she would never, ever wish her beautiful daughter away.

Once the pizza was eaten, they moved to the sofa, where he pulled her close to his side. She relaxed into him, loving the feel of his nearness and the scent of him that stirred her on so many levels.

He turned on a movie they both had wanted to see, but she was more focused on him than the action taking place on his television. As they cuddled together, she stroked her hand back and forth across his broad chest.

It didn't take long for her to sense a growing tension in him. His heartbeat accelerated beneath her touch and his breathing became quickened.

"Being this close to you does terrible things to me, Ainsley," he whispered into her ear.

She raised her head to look at him. "Like what terrible things?"

"You make me think about kissing you until we're both positively breathless. You make me try to imagine what it would be like if I swept you up in my arms, carried you into my bed and made sweet love with you."

Her breath half caught in the back of her throat. "Why, Deputy Churchill, are you trying to seduce me again?"

"I definitely am. How am I doing?" His eyes glittered with the burn of desire.

"You are doing wonderfully well. I'm just wondering why you aren't following your words with actions?"

His lips immediately captured hers in a kiss that seared her right to the bottom of her feet. She was ready to take the next step with Hunter. She was ready to be completely vulnerable and make love with him.

When he finally lifted his lips from hers, she smiled. "Ah, that was good for a beginning, but what happened to the part where you sweep me into your arms and carry me to your bed?"

His eyes widened and then blazed with a passion that only confirmed to her that this was right. It was obvious he wanted her and oh, how she wanted him.

He stood and then picked her up into his arms and walked down the hallway. When he reached his bedroom door, Zeus tried to follow them in.

"Sorry, buddy. This is a party of two." He closed the door to shut the dog out, and then he walked across the room and gently deposited her onto the bed.

He stepped back and gazed at her for a long moment. "I must say, you look amazing in my bed."

"It will be a better picture when you join me here."

He grinned and leaped onto the bed. Her laughter was stolen by another one of his toe-curling kisses. Their tongues swirled together in a heated dance of sensuality.

His hands moved up the back of her blouse, his palms hot against her bare skin. She wanted his hands touching her bare skin everywhere…and she wanted to touch his.

As the kiss ended, she pushed away and sat up and then began unfastening the buttons on her blouse. He sat up as well and watched her. When she was finished with the last button, he reached out and pushed the garment off her shoulders, leaving her clad from the waist up in only her lacy bra. The blouse fell to the bed behind them.

He then grabbed the bottom of his shirt and pulled it off over his head. His bare chest was gorgeous. It was smooth, and his muscles were sculpted and perfect.

They came back together for more kissing and touching, and within minutes her bra went the way of her blouse. Finally, he kicked off his shoes, took off his socks and then shucked his jeans. He looked completely hot clad only in a pair of black boxers.

He moved next to her and unfastened the button on her jeans and then unzipped them. She raised her hips to help him pull them off her, and then there was nothing between them except his boxers and her lacy, pale pink panties.

"You are so beautiful," he whispered. "And I want you so badly."

"Show me," she replied half breathlessly.

He pulled her back into his arms for a deep kiss. After several minutes he slid his lips to kiss behind her ear and then on down her throat.

He melted her with the flames of desire in his eyes, with the heat of his lips and hands on her. When his mouth captured one of her taut nipples, she couldn't help but moan with the sweet sensations.

Her hands gripped his shoulders as he licked and nipped at first one nipple and then the other. This was what she'd wanted…this complete and total closeness with him.

As his hand slid down her stomach to the waistband of her panties, her breath caught in her throat. He slowly moved his fingers from left to right, teasing her and heightening her need for him.

She reached down and found him fully aroused within his boxers. She plucked at the material, wanting the boxers off him so she could stroke his bare hardness.

Before that could happen, his fingers slid beneath her panties and found her moist center. She cried out as electric shocks of pleasure ripped through her. His fingers moved with just the right pressure, with just the right tempo. Her need climbed higher and higher, and then a climax shattered her.

She cried out his name and reached for his arousal once again. "I need more, Hunter," she gasped. "I want you inside me."

He rolled away from her and took off his boxers. He then reached into his nightstand and grabbed a condom. He quickly rolled it on and then positioned himself between her thighs.

He slowly eased into her and held her gaze. His eyes were like a primal forest, dark and wild. He buried himself in her and then remained unmoving for a long moment.

As he continued to look down at her, she felt connected to him not only physically but also emotionally as well. It was as if their souls were uniting as well as their bodies.

Slowly he began to stroke into her, and the tension inside her began to build once again. Their breaths became pants as he increased the quickness of his strokes. She was lost in him...in them.

She'd never felt these incredible feelings before, certainly not in all the years of her marriage. This was more intense, more meaningful, and while he masterfully took control, there was also a wealth of gentleness coming from him.

With a gasp, she felt another climax begin to build inside her. She urged him faster and met each of his thrusts with her own. She felt him surging inside her and the tension stiffening his entire body right before he climaxed sent her back over the edge again.

After several seconds he rolled off her and onto his back next to her. It took a few minutes for them to both catch their breaths.

He propped himself up on an elbow and smiled down at her. "That was better than in my best dreams," he said.

"For me, too."

He reached out and stroked his fingers across an old scar on her abdomen. "What's this from?"

"Oh, uh, a splenectomy due to a car accident," she said. The lie tripped from her lips and she hated herself for it. She still had her spleen, no thanks to Peter, who had tried to kill her by stabbing her to death. Thankfully all the other wounds and broken bones she'd received from him were no longer visible.

Once again he stroked his fingers over the old scar. "I'm sorry that happened to you."

"It was a long time ago," she replied. She sighed and looked at the clock on his nightstand. "It's almost time for you to get me back home."

"I thought it was women who always wanted to bask in the afterglow," he said teasingly. He leaned over and kissed her tenderly.

When the kiss ended, he swept a strand of her long hair away from her face and frowned. "I wish you could stay right here for the whole night. I would love to cuddle you all night long and then wake up in the morning with you in my arms."

She sighed with wistfulness. "I would love that, too, but unfortunately reality intrudes and we need to get up."

"Go ahead and use my master bathroom, I'll use the one in the hallway." He rolled off his side of the bed, grabbed his boxers, jeans and shirt from the floor and then left the bedroom.

Ainsley grabbed her clothing from the bed and the floor and then went into the adjoining bathroom. As her heart finally found a normal rhythm, she dressed and then stared at her reflection in the mirror.

She looked like and felt like a woman who had just been thoroughly loved. Making love to Hunter had been magical. This evening, this experience, had just confirmed what she'd seen coming...she was falling head over heels in love with Hunter Churchill.

She wanted this relationship to thrive and grow. She wanted this healthy and happy relationship. She desperately wanted a future with Hunter. Right now she felt as if it was within her fingertips—she just hoped nothing happened to mess it all up.

Chapter Six

"Deputy Churchill, somebody is out here to see you," Lanie said when she stuck her head into the bullpen.

He gazed at her quizzically, but before he could ask her who, she disappeared again. "Ainsley?" Nick said from his desk.

Hunter shrugged. "She's never shown up here before." But they hadn't spent the kind of night they had shared last night before.

He'd spent far too much of the morning thinking about how much he'd loved the taste of her, the feel of her bare silky skin against his and the evocative scent of her.

He sprang to his feet and hurried to the door. "Go get her, tiger." Nick's laughter chased behind him.

Hunter stepped out into the reception area, disappointed not to see Ainsley but surprised to see Marybeth Wilson. "Marybeth, your dad doing okay?" he asked, instantly concerned about George.

She was a petite blonde and had an aluminum foil–wrapped platter in her hand. "He's doing fine. I should have done this before now, but I wanted to thank you for taking care of him while I was gone. He told me how kind you were to him." She held out the platter. "These are homemade chocolate chip cookies fresh out of the oven."

"Marybeth, you didn't have to do this," he said as he took the platter from her. He made an instant decision not to tell her about his father's visit to his home with his cookies. George apparently hadn't told her, and Hunter wasn't going to rat him out.

She smiled. "Trust me, I needed to do this. You've been so kind to my father on so many occasions. It was about time I did something to show my appreciation."

Hunter smiled. "These cookies smell delicious, but still, I was only doing my job."

"We both know that you have gone above and beyond just doing your job for him many times. Anyway, enjoy the cookies." She gave him another smile and then turned and left.

"You'd better give me one of those cookies before you take them back to the other guys," Lanie said. She jumped out of her chair, ripped the aluminum foil off the cookie plate and then sighed with pleasure. "Look at them…all warm and gooey with chocolate chips." She grabbed two off the platter and then returned to her desk.

"This was really nice," Hunter said.

"Way better than that time Betty Simon brought you her special cauliflower casserole," Lanie replied.

"Yeah, her thoughtfulness was appreciated even if

her cooking skills weren't," Hunter said with a laugh. He returned to his desk, where Nick immediately grabbed two of the cookies. "If these are from Ainsley, then you better marry that girl," he said after a bite.

"Actually, they're from Marybeth Wilson for me taking care of George whenever he goes off the rails. But I am considering marrying Ainsley."

Nick paused with the cookie halfway to his mouth. "Seriously, dude?"

"Seriously," Hunter replied. He didn't know exactly when he'd realized he was completely in love with Ainsley, but he had reached a point in their relationship that love for her filled his heart. Making love with her last night had just confirmed it.

"So, are you going to propose to her soon?"

Hunter frowned. "Not yet. We've got a major issue we need to get past before I'll ask her."

"What's the issue?"

"Her daughter hates me."

Nick's dark brows danced upward in surprise. "Seriously? She hates the most well-liked deputy in the entire county? What did you do to her?"

Hunter laughed. "Nothing. I bought her a stuffed pink unicorn, thinking that would break the ice between us."

"So apparently she isn't into unicorns," Nick said.

"Oh, she was into the unicorn, she just wasn't into me. I'm hoping it's just going to take a little time."

Nick took a bite of the cookie. "Good luck with that, man."

Minutes later Hunter was back patrolling the streets, but his mind was still filled with Ainsley and Melinda. He hoped Dr. Atkins would be able to sort things out with Melinda and the little girl would give him a chance to be a part of her life. Without that, he knew there was no hope for a future with Ainsley.

Still, last night had confirmed to him that she felt close to him. He didn't believe she was the kind of woman who would go to bed with him if she wasn't falling in love with him, and that excited him for the future.

When it was time for his lunch break, he was more than happy to head to the café. He stepped inside, grateful that as usual the lunch rush had passed and the café was relatively quiet.

He spied Ainsley by the soda machine, and he slid into a seat at one of her tables. When she turned around, her beautiful smile lit up her features. She delivered a soda to one of the other diners and then walked over to his table.

"I've been waiting all day to see you," she said.

"That's funny, I've been waiting all day to see you, too," he replied.

"I couldn't wait to thank you, although you shouldn't have." Her eyes twinkled brightly.

"You're welcome, but what is it I shouldn't have done?"

"You know…the roses," she replied with one of her charming blushes rising up to color her cheeks.

"Uh…what roses?"

"Stop playing," she replied and gave him a playful

smack on his shoulder. "They were delivered in here this morning."

He gazed at her solemnly. "Ainsley, I'm not playing with you. I didn't send you roses. What exactly was delivered to you this morning?"

"A dozen red roses in a beautiful vase with no card. I just assumed after last night…" Her voice trailed off.

"I wish I had sent you roses, Ainsley, but I didn't." He reared back in his chair and then grinned at her. "So, it looks like you have a secret admirer and I have some competition."

A deep frown cut across her forehead. "It isn't funny. I don't like secrets."

"I'm sure if you give it a little time whoever sent them to you will let you know."

"I hope you're right," she replied. Her frown smoothed out somewhat. "Now, what can I get you for lunch?"

He placed his order with her, missing the flirtatious small talk they usually indulged in. He watched her taking care of the other diners in her section, and a sense of disquiet suddenly filled him. Despite the way Ainsley had reacted to the roses, maybe he shouldn't be so sure of himself when it came to her.

Who in the hell was her secret admirer, and how much did he have to worry about him?

AINSLEY SAT AT her kitchen table and stared at the vase of red roses that had been delivered to her in the café that morning.

When she'd realized the gorgeous roses beautifully arranged in a white vase were for her, she'd been thrilled. She'd also been certain they had been from Hunter even though there hadn't been a card.

Lana had teased her unmercifully, and the other waitresses, both married and single, had looked at her with a bit of envy. She'd quickly carried them back to her kitchen table and then had hurried back to the floor to continue working.

She'd spent the rest of the morning anticipating seeing Hunter and then when she had and he'd told her he hadn't sent the roses, a sick feeling had swept through her.

She definitely didn't like surprises. She'd had enough of them during her marriage to Peter. She'd never known whether he was going to stroke her hair or pull it, smile at her or smack her. The secrets that only he could hear and see in his own head kept him unpredictable and dangerous.

She shook her head to dispel any further thoughts of Peter. She couldn't allow herself to be pulled back into memories of his brutality and utter madness.

If not Hunter, then who had sent her the roses? The longer she stared at them, the higher her anxiety climbed. They were such a deep red…like the color of blood.

Now why would she think that? The flowers might represent a special thank-you to her or a budding romantic interest from somebody. She just wished the sender had sent an identifying card as well.

She glanced at the clock. It was just after eight. There was only one flower shop in town, and they might still be open. Maybe she could get some answers from somebody there.

She found the number and then called. "April's Flowers," a pleasant female voice answered. "This is Megan speaking, how can I help you?"

"Hi, Megan. My name is Ainsley Meadows, and I work at the Dusty Gulch Café. This morning a dozen red roses were delivered to me there, and I was wondering if you could tell me who sent them."

"I'd love to help you out, but there was no order for a dozen roses that came out of my shop today," Megan said.

Ainsley paused in surprise. "Are you sure?"

The woman on the other end of the line laughed. "Honey, I've been here all day, and a sale for roses is a good day for me. Trust me, no roses went out today or any time in the last few weeks."

"Thank you anyway," Ainsley said. She hung up and then stared at the roses again. She hadn't paid much attention to the young man who had delivered them. He'd worn a hat, so she didn't even know if he'd been blond or brunette.

She jerked up from the table and carried the roses to the trash can. If they weren't from Hunter, then she didn't want them. The flowers finished filling the trash bag, and she tied it at the top and then carried it to her door.

The dumpster for the café was just at the back of

the property. She regularly carried her trash bags out to it, but for some reason she was particularly on edge tonight.

You can always take the trash out tomorrow when there's more daylight, a little voice whispered in her head. *You've taken the trash out at this time of night a hundred times before*, another voice chided.

Irritated with herself, she unlocked the door, grabbed the trash bag and stepped outside. The cool night air wrapped itself around her as she scurried across the parking lot toward the dumpster.

The night seemed deeper…darker than usual as the moon was covered by clouds. The streetlamp on the corner provided only the faintest illumination into this area.

She reached the dumpster and threw in her bag. A rustling behind the dumpster froze her in her tracks. Was somebody there? Was somebody hiding behind the trash receptacle? Watching her? Waiting for her?

Her heart began to pound as she took a step backward, keeping her gaze shooting from the dumpster to the area just around it. Somebody had sent her roses… was it possible that somebody was stalking her?

She jumped and released a sudden laugh in relief as a mouse scurried out from behind the dumpster and raced across the parking lot. Jeez, what was wrong with her?

She went back inside the apartment and sank down on the sofa. She was being ridiculous. Just because she'd gotten roses from an unknown person didn't mean that something was wrong…that something was somehow threatening.

Hunter was right—somebody would probably come forward by the end of the next day to claim the roses and say why they had sent them to her.

Her negative reaction was from her past. Peter had always gotten her roses…sometimes as an apology for beating her, and sometimes in anticipation of beating her. But Peter wasn't around. And hopefully he had no idea where she was. Most men would assume any woman loved that particular flower.

She had just gotten into bed when her phone rang. She saw the caller identification and immediately answered, unable to halt the smile that curved her lips.

"I've decided I love the sound of your voice right before I go to sleep," Hunter said.

"Same," she replied simply.

"I've been kicking myself all day long," he said.

"Why is that?"

"After last night I should have been the one to send you roses."

"Hunter, making love to you was all the gift I needed. I don't need you to send me roses or gifts. You're all I want."

"God, I'm crazy about you," he replied.

She laughed. "You're just happy because I'm a cheap date."

"Well, there is that," he returned with a laugh of his own. "I just wanted to tell you to have sweet dreams."

"Thank you, Hunter. Sweet dreams to you, too."

Her smile continued to ride her lips long after the phone call ended. Making love with Hunter had been like fulfilling a fantasy. He'd been so gentle, so wonderfully tender and everything she had hoped he would be.

She awakened the next morning feeling well rested and more centered. She was especially pleased that over breakfast Melinda didn't mention hearing her father talk to her the night before. Maybe the appointment with Dr. Atkins was already making a difference.

Since it was Saturday, Melinda settled in at a small two-top table next to the kitchen with Ainsley's phone for playing games, a pack of crayons and several coloring books, and colored pencils with drawing paper. Melinda was always good about keeping herself occupied on Saturdays when Ainsley worked and Melinda was out of school.

As Ainsley started her workday, she couldn't help but speculate about the sender of the roses. When she told Lana that Hunter hadn't sent them to her and the local florist hadn't delivered them, Lana played sleuth with her.

"Maybe Jim Nelson sent them to you," Lana said when the Ainsley met her at the coffee machine. "You know that man thinks the world of you."

Ainsley thought of the elderly man who she served breakfast to each morning. "He's a sweet man, but I don't see him sending me roses for getting his order right each day. Besides, he also doesn't strike me as a man who has that kind of money to throw away. I'm sure a dozen roses aren't cheap."

"That's true. Hell, most of the men in this town wouldn't spend the money to send a woman a dozen daisies. Bunch of cheapskates, if you ask me," Lana grumbled and then brightened. "What about Jimmy Miller? You know that boy makes a good salary working for Eva and Jake Albright, and he definitely acts like he might have a crush on you."

"Lana, order up," Big Ed hollered, effectively halting their conversation.

Was it possible Jimmy had sent the flowers to her? He was definitely a flirt when he came in. He also always sat in her section. The more she thought about it, the more convinced she was that Jimmy had bought her the roses. He'd told her that Hunter was a hard man to challenge…was he attempting to do just that by sending her the flowers? When he came in for lunch today, he'd probably confess that he'd sent them.

She smiled when George Calvert walked in with another man she didn't recognize. The two remained standing and talking to each other just inside the door. She assumed the two were together, but then George took a seat in her section and the other man sat in Lana's.

"Hi, George," she said. "For a minute I thought you would be sitting at a table for two with a friend."

"Nah, I just met that gentleman outside the door. He's new in town and his name is Hank Bridges,"

George replied. "He's single and bought the old pig farm just outside the city limits."

"Well, it's nice to see you again," she said. "You look good."

"I'm feeling pretty good. I decided I needed one of Big Ed's breakfast specials this morning."

"Would you like the one with the pancakes or the biscuits and gravy?"

"I have a hankering for pancakes, so I'll take the special that includes them."

"And to drink?"

"A cup of coffee will be just fine."

"I'll put your order in and get your coffee right away."

Ainsley placed George's order and then once again met Lana at the coffee machine. "Don't look now, but the new man in town has been checking you out," Lana said. "I swear, Ainsley, you could have your pick of a dozen single men in town."

Ainsley laughed. "I've got the single man I want."

"And a good one he is," Lana replied.

Suddenly Ainsley was reminded of what Juanita had said about Hunter's past, something Hunter hadn't shared with her yet. Everything had been going so well with Hunter, she'd forgotten what Juanita had said.

What could it be that Hunter hadn't told her yet? They'd shared so many conversations, shared so many things about each other. What might he be hiding? And was it something that might play a negative role in their relationship?

Ha, she was worried about him having secrets when she probably had more secrets than anyone else in town. Definitely double standards. She expected him to come clean about everything while she was lying to him about almost everything.

As she served George his coffee, she glanced over to the new man in town. The single ladies should be happy with a new, attractive man in town.

His dark brown hair was nicely cut, and he had high cheekbones and a perfectly straight nose. When he smiled at Lana, his teeth were straight and white... altogether he was quite a hunk.

But, despite his good looks, he stirred absolutely nothing in her. Her heart was already completely taken by a very hot deputy sheriff named Hunter.

The breakfast rush passed, and then it seemed like just a minute went by and the lunch rush was on. Ainsley scooted from table to table along with Lana and two other waitresses who worked on the weekends.

"How's the best-looking waitress in the county doing today?" Jimmy Miller greeted her with his usual smile when she arrived to take his order.

"I'm doing just fine. What about you?" If he'd been the one who had sent her the roses, surely he'd say something about them now.

"I'm doing pretty good, although it sounds like we're supposed to get some nasty wet days next week."

"I hate to see the weather turning cold," she replied.

"Me too. Winters in Dusty Gulch can sometimes be pretty brutal," he replied.

"What can I get for you, Jimmy?"

He ordered, and if he was the one who had sent her the roses, apparently he wasn't ready to confess to her yet. If not Jimmy, then who? The question continued to haunt her.

With a pause in the patrons, Ainsley went over to Melinda's table. "Hey love bug, are you ready to order some lunch?"

"Yes, but first look at the picture I drew for you." Melinda scooted over a picture of a pink house with lots of purple flowers amid a bright green lawn.

"That's awesome, honey."

"Do you think we could find a pink house for our forever house?" Melinda asked.

"It might be easier to plant pretty pink flowers in front of our forever house. Would that be okay, too?" Melinda nodded. "Now, tell me what you'd like for lunch."

"Grilled cheese with chips," Melinda said.

"How about grilled cheese with an apple?"

"Okay," Melinda replied. "But I'd rather have chips."

"Maybe tomorrow you can have chips," Ainsley said. "While you wait for your lunch, I want you to think if maybe you could give Hunter another chance if we all go out for pizza. We can talk more about it later this evening."

Once Melinda was finished with her lunch, she returned to the apartment to watch television. She knew the rules as far as keeping the door locked and not answering it if anyone knocked.

While they'd been in town with Ainsley working the hours she did, she and Melinda had fallen into a good routine for Saturdays.

Melinda spent the mornings in the café and then got to watch television in the afternoons until Ainsley got off work before the Saturday evening rush. Throughout the afternoon it was easy for Ainsley to step into the back to check on her daughter.

Hunter came in for his lunch break, and as usual, he flirted with her as she took his order and then served his meal. "I'm hoping maybe Thursday we could try to do pizza with Melinda," she said.

He looked at her in pleased surprise. "That would be nice. I'm willing to do and try whatever to make her like me. Maybe I should get her a pink teddy bear."

"No more gifts for her," she said sternly. "I don't want you trying to buy her affection."

She didn't hang around for more conversation with him. The café continued to stay too busy for chitchat. "Fifteen more minutes and then the two of us can get out of here," Lana said as the two stood side by side and watched the diners. "You have any plans for the rest of the weekend?"

"Tomorrow I'll probably take Melinda for a drive around town just to get out of the apartment for a little while. We'll shop a bit and then wind up at the ice cream parlor for a treat," Ainsley said. "What about you?"

"I figure it's time for me to do a changeover in my closet. You know, pack away the summer clothes and pull out the winter," Lana replied. "In other words, I'm going to have a damned boring day."

"Sometimes boring is good, especially after the busy day we've had here today."

"Hey, Ainsley." Rhonda Carlton, one of the waitresses who had come in to work the dinner rush, hurried toward her.

"Hi, Rhonda. What's up?" Ainsley's smile faded as Rhonda didn't offer her one in return.

"Uh…I was cleaning off the table back by the restrooms and I found this." Rhonda's blue eyes were troubled as she held out a folded piece of paper.

For a moment Ainsley didn't want to take it from her. The look in Rhonda's eyes scared her. Finally she took the note and opened it. A frightened gasp escaped her as she read the bold block letters.

AINSLEY MEADOWS. YOU ARE A WHORE AND WE DON'T LIKE WHORES IN THIS TOWN.

Chapter Seven

Hunter held the offending note in his gloved hand. Around him the sounds of people laughing and glasses clinking sounded like a normal Saturday night in the café.

But this note wasn't normal, and he hated to see the fear that kept Ainsley's eyes darkened. "How about we go into your apartment where things will be quieter," he suggested.

"Okay," Ainsley agreed.

He looked at Rhonda. "If you could come back with us, I'll just keep you off the floor for a minute or two."

Rhonda shot a look at Big Ed and then looked back at Hunter. "Can't I just talk to you right here? My section is full of people."

"Okay, just tell me exactly where you found the note," Hunter said.

She pointed to a two-top table in the back. "It was just sitting there. I thought it was just somebody's trash, but then I opened it." She frowned. "I don't even know who has sat at that table today. I had just come in for work when I found it."

"Thank you," Hunter said. "I may need to talk to you later, okay?"

Rhonda nodded. "Can I get back to work now?"

"Yes, that's fine." Hunter turned back to Ainsley. "Let's get out of here."

She led the way through the door that entered into her apartment. "Melinda, could you please go play in your bedroom for a little while? I need to talk to Deputy Churchill."

Once Melinda was gone, Hunter gestured Ainsley toward her small dining table. He placed the note into an evidence bag he'd carried into the café when he'd arrived and then set the bag down.

"What's happening, Hunter? Why would somebody leave that note for me?"

"Did you have any problems with anyone today while you were working?" he asked. He hated the tension that wafted from her and the simmer of fear in her eyes.

"No…nobody. It was a good day. First the roses and now this… What is going on? Why is somebody doing this to me?"

"I don't know, but I'm going to figure it out." He pulled off his gloves and then reached across the table to cover her hands. They were icy cold. He rubbed them in an attempt to warm them, even though he knew their coldness had nothing to do with an outside chill.

"I just can't imagine who would think such a terrible thing about me. What have I done that would give anyone the impression that I'm a whore?"

"Nothing…absolutely nothing," Hunter replied. "Ainsley, I don't want you to overreact to this. It's not a threatening note, it's just a nasty one, and I'm going to do my very best to try to figure out who left it."

She pulled her hands from his and instead wrapped her arms around herself. "Whore…that's what my husband used to call me when he was angry with me."

"Well, then he was a nasty man, too. But as far as I know, your ex-husband is nowhere around. Was Ben Wilkins in to eat today?"

"He was in for lunch. He seemed sober and he sat in Lana's section."

"Then I'll be having a chat with him today. Do you remember who sat at that specific table during the day?"

She frowned. "I don't think anyone did. We try not to seat anyone there unless we absolutely have to. It's so close to the restrooms."

"So it would be easy for anyone who went to the restroom to just drop the note on the table," he said.

She nodded. "And that's going to make it impossible to find out who left it," she replied. "It's probably not even a crime."

"That doesn't mean I'm not going to investigate it," Hunter countered. "But you're right. No crime has been committed, and at least the note isn't threatening."

"It's definitely character assassination," she replied darkly.

He laughed. "Honey, anyone who knows you knows what kind of good woman you are, and you are not what that note said. That note was just somebody venting in a childish manner. It definitely sounds like something Ben Wilkins might do."

Hunter rose from the table and then pulled her up into his arms. She remained stiff against him for a long minute and then released a deep sigh and rested her head against his chest.

He stroked her hair, and when she looked up at him he kissed her gently. After the kiss, he held her gaze. "I don't want you to worry about this. I don't want you to give it any more thought. Deal?"

She hesitated a moment and then nodded. "Deal."

He released her, and together they walked to the door that would take him outside. "Now, before I leave, can I see one of your sunshine smiles?" he asked.

She smiled, but the gesture didn't quite lighten her eyes. "You'll let me know what you find out?"

"Of course. And even if I don't have any answers, I'll call you before bedtime."

"I'd like that." This time her smile was more relaxed.

Once he left he immediately drove back to the station to speak to Sheriff Black. He had a good working relationship with Wayne, mostly because Wayne was a hands-off kind of boss. He trusted the people who worked for him, but Hunter knew Wayne could also be a bit lazy.

Once back he knocked on Wayne's private office door. "Enter," Wayne yelled. "Hunter, isn't it time for you to be heading home?"

"Yeah, but something has come up and I just wanted to discuss it with you."

"Well, sit down and discuss."

Hunter sat in the straight-back chair facing Wayne's desk and explained about the note directed at Ainsley that was found in the café. He relayed his feeling that Ben Wilkins could have left it.

"What I'd like to do is hunt Ben down tonight and question him about it and also question anyone else who might possibly be responsible for it. Naturally it has Ainsley a bit upset."

Wayne frowned. "A nasty note isn't a crime."

"I'm aware of that, and I certainly won't take away any time from my normal duties. Tonight I'll be on my own time, but I just wanted for you to be aware of what I'm doing about this."

Wayne shook his head and then leaned back in his chair and scratched the top of his head. "Why would Ben have it in for Ainsley?"

"He went into the café drunk and disorderly one morning, and she basically had to kick him out."

"I wish when Ben left town a couple of months ago he would have stayed gone."

"That makes two of us," Hunter replied.

"Your plan to do a little sleuthing on the side is fine with me. So, go…get out of here so you can get to it."

"Thanks, Wayne."

Minutes later Hunter was in his patrol car hunting down Ben Wilkins. His first stop was the Dusty Gulch Motel, a sad six-unit that rented out nightly or monthly to whoever would make the choice to live here.

He parked in front of the office and stepped out of his vehicle. The air smelled faintly of marijuana and spoiled garbage, of hopelessness and neglect.

The motel was owned by Jeb Harness. When Hunter entered the office, the old man sat behind the counter reading a tabloid magazine. "Deputy," he said in greeting. He didn't bother to get up. "Who you looking for tonight?"

"Ben Wilkins. What room is he in?"

"What's that drunk done this time?" Jeb asked.

"Just the kinds of things that drunks do," Hunter replied.

Jeb shook his head. "He's in unit three."

"Thanks, Jeb."

Hunter left the office and walked the short distance to Ben's room. No lights shone from the window to indicate that anyone was inside.

Hunter knocked on the door and waited. No answer. He knocked again, this time harder. Still, there was no response. He was just about to knock a third time when the door to unit four opened and Jane Landers, an older woman who also liked her booze, leaned out.

"He ain't there. He took his bottle and went off

somewhere. His stingy butt didn't even want to share with me," she said, her voice slurred enough to let him know she'd been drinking heavily as well.

"Thanks, Jane." At least when she got drunk, she didn't leave her room. She didn't cause issues like Ben often did.

Hunter got back in his car and headed for Main Street. He knew the places where Ben often parked himself to drink his bottle. He didn't find him on the bench in front of the post office or in the doorway of the grocery store.

He did find him seated in the alcove in front of the drugstore. Hunter parked his vehicle, got out and approached him. "Hey, Ben," he said in greeting.

"Ah, Deputy Churchy, are you here to arrest me?" Ben asked, his voice heavily slurred.

"I don't know, Ben. Do you need to be arrested?" Hunter asked.

Ben frowned. "I don't think so. I'm just sitting here not bothering anyone," he replied. "I'm being quiet, so I'm not disturbing the peace."

"That's good, Ben. So tell me, what do you think of Ainsley Meadows?"

Ben's frown deepened. "Who?"

"Ainsley at the café," Hunter said.

"At the café…oh, her." Ben's rheumy eyes narrowed. "She's a mean witch. She doesn't like me and I don't like her. She threw me out of the café just because I was a little bit drunk and a little bit rowdy."

"Did you maybe leave her a nasty note when you were in the café earlier today?" Hunter asked.

"A nasty note?" Ben frowned. "What kind of a nasty note?"

"You tell me," Hunter replied.

Ben's frown creased his forehead again. "I didn't leave no nasty note in the café for her or anyone else."

"You sure about that, Ben?"

"I'm positive," he replied, and then laughed. "Heck, I wouldn't even know where to get a decent piece of paper or a pencil."

Hunter stared at him for several long minutes. He believed him. Despite Ben's inebriated state, there was an innocence shining from his eyes that Hunter believed.

Ben stayed drunk enough most of the time that to believe he'd had the foresight to get a piece of paper and a pen and actually write a note about something that had happened in the past seemed impossible.

As Hunter finally headed home, his thoughts were troubled. When he'd seen the note and heard that Ben had been in the café that morning, he'd been sure that the man had written it in retaliation for Ainsley having him thrown out of the café.

Now, with Ben off the table, the note somehow seemed a bit more ominous. Who might hold such a strong negative feeling toward Ainsley?

It was just a hateful note, he told himself, but there was a small thought that niggled in the back of his head. Was the note the end of it, or was it the beginning of something much bigger, something that might be more dangerous?

LONG AFTER HUNTER had left, a chill continued to fill Ainsley as she thought of the note. Although she succeeded in keeping things normal for the rest of the evening for Melinda's sake, once her daughter was in bed, Ainsley wandered the small space they called home.

She checked to make sure that both doors were locked and then checked the locks on all the windows. She told herself she shouldn't take a stupid, anonymous note so seriously, and yet she couldn't help how much it had unsettled her.

Finally exhausted, she flopped down on the sofa. Her thoughts continued to fly through her head as if a tornado had lodged there.

Who had written the hateful note? Other than Ben Wilkins, whom had she offended so badly? As much as she wanted to believe it had been written for spite by Ben, she found it hard to believe that he'd actually carry a grudge through his alcoholic haze to write it.

If not him, then who?

Or was it possible this had little to do with her and more to do with Hunter? Did the secret Juanita had hinted about have to do with another woman? A woman now displaying an ugly jealousy toward Ainsley?

She mentally picked through everything that had ever happened between her and Hunter, and a new question popped into her head. What was behind the closed door in his house?

Both times she'd been there, all the doors in his house had been wide-open except one. He'd indicated it was just an empty room, but was it? And if it was, then why not keep the door open?

Knowing her thoughts were going way left field, she got up and headed to bed. She'd just changed into her nightgown when her phone rang.

She sat on the edge of the bed and answered. "Hi, Hunter. I hope you have some information for me."

"I wish I had some information for you, but I don't. I caught up with Ben Wilkins and questioned him. He was drunk, but he said he didn't write the note, and unfortunately I believed him."

"So, we're back to square one." Disappointment swept through her.

"I'm going to keep questioning people, but I'm inclined to chalk this up to a juvenile, disgruntled diner and nothing more."

"I've been thinking, and I was wondering if maybe that note wasn't so much about me, but maybe about a woman you dated who sees me as a threat…a woman you haven't told me about."

There was a long moment of silence. "Ainsley, I haven't dated anyone since my divorce. There are no women I'm keeping secret from you."

"I just know Juanita mentioned to me there were things in your past, things that I don't know about and she wouldn't tell me."

Again there was a long pause. "There are some things I still need to share with you, but they aren't things I want to tell you over a phone call. Is it possible for Juanita to watch Melinda tomorrow evening so you could come over here and we can talk?"

"I can probably arrange that. What time is good for you?" A touch of anxiety replaced the disappointment that had filled her when he'd told her Ben wasn't the note writer.

"I'm working tomorrow, so why don't we say around six thirty," he said.

"That should work. Instead of you coming here to pick me up, I'll just drive over to your place." She'd prefer to have her own car to escape in if things somehow went south between them.

"Okay, I'll see you then."

Ainsley hung up and frowned. Whatever he was going to tell her, it must be serious, and that filled her with even more anxiety.

Things had been going so well with Hunter. She should have known there would be a glitch. Right now she just didn't know if the glitch was a deal breaker or not.

Yes, she should have known something would happen to screw up the happiness she'd been living. It was as if the fates refused to allow her to live happily.

The next day she and Melinda headed out for a day of fun, and Ainsley refused to allow thoughts of nasty notes, the mysterious roses and Hunter's secrets to ruin the day.

They took a drive around town, exploring areas they hadn't yet seen. It was a beautiful day, but rain was supposed to move in later in the evening.

At lunchtime they went into one of the two drive-through hamburger places in town. Once again that morning Melinda hadn't mentioned her father "talk-ing" to her.

Ainsley certainly didn't intend to bring it up, but she and Melinda hadn't had a chance to talk about Hunter. "I asked you yesterday about you giving Hunter an-other chance," Ainsley said. "Have you thought about it?"

Melinda dragged one of her fries through a puddle of ketchup and then popped it into her mouth. At the same time she nodded and chewed.

"So, you have thought about it?" Ainsley pressed.

"Yeah. I guess I could give him a chance. Even though Daddy doesn't like him, I know he makes you happy, and I did like the unicorn he bought for me."

"So, if we all went out for pizza this Thursday night, you could be nice to him?"

"I could be nice," Melinda agreed. "But if Daddy comes for me, I want to go with him for a while. I'd come back to be with you again after I'm with Daddy for a little while. That's only fair."

Ainsley bit her tongue, not wanting to ruin the day by arguing with her daughter. What Melinda didn't know was if Peter ever got hold of her, he would never let her go.

Peter didn't want a daughter. He wanted a possession he could control. He wanted Melinda solely to hurt Ainsley, and she would die before she allowed Peter anywhere near Melinda. The scar on her stomach suddenly burned, reminding her that she'd nearly died at Peter's hands before.

After eating lunch they went into a clothing store that sold children's fashions as well as women's. Even though it was Sunday, the stores along Main Street were all open for business. They bought Melinda two new sweaters and a cute pair of jeans, and Ainsley bought herself a lightweight turquoise sweater to wear later that evening with Hunter.

She'd already talked to Juanita about babysitting for a couple of hours, and Melinda was looking forward to spending some time with her friends.

They ate an early dinner at the Red Wok and then topped off the day with a stop at the ice cream parlor. It was after five when they got home, and Ainsley immediately began to get ready to go to Hunter's house.

She'd managed to stay out of her own head for most of the day, but now her anxiety returned. What did Hunter have to share with her and how might whatever he told her affect their relationship? First the roses, then the ugly note and now this. What was going on in her world?

An hour later as she was on her way to his house, the level of love she had for Hunter slammed into her and nearly brought tears to her eyes.

He was the man she'd been waiting for…a man who treated her with respect, a man who made her feel protected and loved. She'd fantasized about a man like him, had spent many nights dreaming that a man like Hunter would appear in her life.

She'd believed she was marrying a good man who loved her when she'd married Peter. She'd had no idea what kind of a monster he was. Her dream of happily-ever-after had quickly become a horrendous nightmare.

She believed Hunter was the real deal. Looking back, there had been a lot of red flags where Peter was concerned, but she'd seen no such red flags with Hunter. Now that he was in her life and her heart was so involved, she feared something was going to happen to spoil it all.

And she had a terrible feeling that tonight might be the night it all fell apart.

Chapter Eight

Hunter paced the length of his living room as he waited for Ainsley to arrive. He probably should have told her more about his past before now, but he hadn't really spoken about the loss of his baby boy to anyone.

He wasn't ashamed of his grief—he'd just held it tightly inside him. But now it was time for him to share. Part of that sharing meant not only allowing himself to be more vulnerable than he'd ever been, but also showing himself as being stupid and incredibly naive.

It was time. It was past time. He wanted to be one hundred percent open and honest with her. Tonight he was putting it all on the line for her. He was going to share his sorrow with her and hope she didn't see him as a weak man.

At exactly six thirty, his doorbell rang. He opened the door, and as always his breath caught at the sight of her. She was absolutely stunning in a pair of jeans and a turquoise sweater that enhanced the bright blue of her eyes.

"Come on in." He stepped aside so she could step into the entry. "Why don't you have a seat on the sofa."

"Thanks," she replied.

"Want something to drink? I have wine and soda."

"No, thanks, I'm good." She settled in on the sofa, and he sank down next to her.

"Is it raining yet?"

She shook her head, her beautiful long hair rippling with the movement. "The skies are definitely clouding up, but so far no rain. Hunter, I don't want to talk about the weather. I've been worried all day that you have secrets that are going to tear us apart. I really care about you."

"Ainsley, I don't have any deep, dark secrets. I know what Juanita was probably referring to, and it's time I share it with you so you know all the pieces of me and my past." He rose and held out his hand to her. "Come with me."

He took her down the hallway to the bedroom that held his tears. He drew a deep breath and then opened the door and turned on the light.

She pulled her hand from his and looked around the room and then up at him in obvious confusion. "What is this, Hunter? Do...do you have a child?"

"I used to." He waited for the soul-wrenching sorrow to overtake him, but the ragged, rough edges of grief had finally softened.

"Did your wife get custody of him?" she asked.

"No, God got custody."

She stared at him for several long moments and then took a step toward him. "Oh Hunter, what happened?"

"Let's go back to the living room to talk." He didn't want to talk about Danny here in the room where the little boy had spent part of his short life.

They returned to the sofa, and this time she sat close to his side, her warmth and familiar scent a balm to him as he dived into the pain of his past.

"We didn't plan for Emily to get pregnant so quickly after we got married, but despite our precautions, it happened. I was thrilled. All I'd ever wanted was to be a deputy and to have a family." He paused a moment, trying to swallow against the emotion that rose up inside him.

As if she sensed his sudden struggle, she reached out and took one of his hands in hers. Her gaze was soft and gave him the strength to continue.

"I was thrilled when Danny was born. He was the most perfect little boy. He was such a happy baby. He rarely fussed, and I would have given my life for him." Hunter's chest tightened.

"When he had just turned a year old, we discovered he had leukemia. For the next year, he was in and out of the hospital for chemo, and we'd hoped that he'd beat it. But just after his second birthday, we lost him."

"Oh Hunter. I'm so very sorry. I can't even imagine the pain of losing a child." She squeezed his hand and then leaned closer and wrapped her arms around his neck.

He pulled her close and buried his face in her sweet-smelling hair. He found comfort in her embrace. He'd grieved so long and so hard all alone. It was oddly soothing to share this horrible event in his life with her.

Tears burned at his eyes, but he swallowed against them. He had already shed more than enough tears over losing Danny.

He finally released her. "I've heard that the loss of a child often causes a divorce," she said. "Is that what happened to you and your wife?"

"No, although certainly we did grieve separately, but I had every intention to try to make the marriage work after Danny was gone. Unfortunately, she didn't. The same day we buried our son, she told me she'd been having an affair since the day we got married and she wasn't even sure Danny was mine."

Ainsley gasped. "What kind of a woman was she? To do that to you? To do that to any man at a time like that." Anger fired in her eyes.

"It didn't matter. That little boy was mine the moment a nurse handed him to me after his birth. She couldn't take that away from me, no matter what she said or what she had done."

"Love is what makes a child yours, not genetics," she replied fervently.

"Another point of pain was I guess everyone in town except me knew that Emily was cheating on me. In retrospect, the signs were all there. She was often unavailable to me. She never let me see her phone. There were dozens of flags…I just didn't want to see any of them."

"Hunter, I'm so very sorry for you." Sympathy replaced the momentary anger in her gaze. "You deserved so much better than that, and I'm so sorry you had to go through so much."

"I have no other secrets, Ainsley. I was just afraid if I told you about all this, you would somehow see me differently."

"Differently how?" She looked at him curiously.

"I don't know…I thought you'd somehow see me as weak and stupid," he confessed.

"Oh Hunter. Rather than making you look weak and stupid, all this makes you look incredibly strong and compassionate and loving. It takes a strong man to shed tears, to be vulnerable with his emotions."

Once again he pulled her into his arms and held her close. The sound of rain began to patter at the windows as if it were his tears for Danny.

Still, there was a new peace inside him where his past was concerned. There would always be sadness in his heart when he thought of his little boy, but he was truly ready to move on from that and seek new happiness in his life.

He leaned back from her. "Maybe one day you could come over and help me pack away the last of the items in Danny's room."

"Are you sure you're ready to do that?" Her gaze was incredibly soft.

He nodded. "Actually, it's past time. I don't need the things to remember him. Besides, maybe someday in the future it would make a great bedroom for a little girl."

"That would be nice in time," she replied. "But of course I'll come over and help you whenever you're ready."

"Thanks, Ainsley, and I promise there are no more secrets in my life."

"I'm glad you shared with me." She smiled at him. "While I waited to talk to you this evening, I'd almost convinced myself that you had an insane wife locked up in that room—although your wife had to have been insane to cheat on you."

He laughed. "Ainsley, you are good for my heart and soul."

She held his gaze for a long moment. "Hunter, I...I..." She looked down and then back up at him. "I...I probably need to get back home since I have Melinda at Juanita's on an unexpected night." She stood from the sofa.

"I really appreciate you coming over tonight." He got up as well to walk her to the door. "And I really hate to send you out in the rain."

"It's not raining that hard, and I don't melt when wet," she replied with another one of her smiles. She stood on her tiptoes and gave him a kiss on the cheek. "Thank you for sharing with me tonight, Hunter."

"Thank you for your caring and support." He opened the front door and peered out into the dark, rainy night. "Why don't you call me so I know you got home safely?"

"I can do that," she replied.

"At least let me get you an umbrella."

"That's not necessary. I'll be fine. I'll call you when I get home." With those words she stepped outside and hurried to her car.

He watched until she backed out of his driveway, and then her car lights disappeared, swallowed by the darkness of the rainy night.

He finally closed the door and with his cell phone in hand, he went back into Danny's room. The sorrow that had lived here was now tempered by the scent of Ainsley that lingered, by the support of her caring arms around him.

Yes, it was time to pack away the items in this room and put his past truly behind him. He no longer needed these things to remind him of what he'd gone through. Ainsley was partially responsible for him moving on and looking forward instead of backward.

He left the bedroom and returned to the living room. He sank down on the sofa and checked the time. The rain was now coming down in torrents, although there was no thunder or lightning. He hoped Ainsley remembered to call him when she got home.

There had been a moment when he'd thought she was going to tell him something, but then she apparently changed her mind. What might she have to share with him? He pushed that moment out of his head. If she did have something to tell him, then hopefully, eventually she would.

He still hoped to get to the bottom of the roses that had been sent to her and the nasty note left at the café.

Both left a bad taste in his mouth and unsettled him, and he knew she was worried about the same things.

He wouldn't feel better until he solved the mystery of who had sent the flowers and left the note. It was so odd, to get beautiful roses and then the horrible note. Were they from a single person or two separate people? Once again he wondered if and when something more might happen, and if there would be a dangerous escalation?

SHE'D ALMOST TOLD HIM. There had been a moment when she'd been comforting him that Ainsley had wanted to come clean and tell him the truth about herself. But the moment had passed without her confessing anything.

Did she really have to tell him anything? The people from the battered-women underground had assured her that her new identity would stand up under any scrutiny. Could she go forward with Hunter and never tell him the truth?

She didn't believe she could. But she had to pick the perfect time to tell him about Peter and how she had violated a child custody order and gone on the run.

She felt like she just needed a little more time. She wanted to see if her daughter would come around where Hunter was concerned—once she did, then it would be time for Ainsley to come clean with Hunter.

The rain pelted her car window as she drove down Main Street, making visibility difficult. But it was easy to see the car lights that fell in too close behind her.

She frowned. It was too dark for her to be able to tell what kind or color of car followed her. Were they actually following her? Or was it just a coincidence that somebody was driving so close to her?

Her heart beat an uneven rhythm as she tightened her fingers around the steering wheel. Was it possible the person who had left the nasty note was behind her right now? Were they going to run her off the road? Try to get her out of her car?

She shuddered with relief as the car turned off on a side street and disappeared from her sight. She released a deep sigh. God, she had gotten herself so worked up, and it had probably just been somebody in a hurry to get home in the rain.

The next couple of days passed without incident. Hunter told her he was still hunting down the sender of the roses and the note, but she knew he had nothing to go on and so was expecting no real results.

She now sat in Dr. Atkins's office, waiting for Melinda to get finished with her latest therapy session. On the way over Melinda had told her mother that Peter had stopped talking to her every night, but he still talked to her every other night or so. Ainsley hoped that this was a sign that slowly Melinda was giving up the fantasy of her father talking to her at night.

Tomorrow she, Hunter and Melinda were set to go out for pizza, and Ainsley definitely didn't want any repeat of the last time the two people she cared about had tried to spend time together.

Dr. Atkins had spoken to Ainsley first to see how

things had gone over the past week. Ainsley had told her that for the most part Melinda had stopped talking about Peter, but Ainsley wasn't sure if that meant Melinda was putting away the fantasy or if she'd simply stopped sharing with Ainsley.

Forty minutes later Dr. Atkins and Melinda walked out. Once again they were both smiling, and Ainsley felt herself relax. "If you don't mind, I'll call you later in the week to touch base with you," Dr. Atkins said to Ainsley. "Unfortunately I've had an emergency come up, and I need to leave right now and head to the hospital."

"Then I'll talk to you later and we're out of here," Ainsley replied.

"How are you feeling?" Ainsley asked once she and Melinda were in the car.

"Good, but I'd feel better if we went to get ice cream."

Ainsley laughed. "Is this going to be a thing every time we see Dr. Atkins?"

Melinda giggled. "Yeah," she replied.

"Then I guess we're going to get ice cream." Ainsley would have liked to hear from Dr. Atkins after she'd spoken to Melinda, but she'd just have to wait to hear from the doctor. Although her first instinct was to ask Melinda all kinds of questions, she refrained from doing so.

While the two ate their ice cream, Melinda talked about school and the friends she had made since they'd been in Dusty Gulch.

"Don't forget that tomorrow night we're going out to the pizza place with Hunter," Ainsley said.

"I know, and I told you I'll behave," Melinda replied.

"Honestly, Melinda, Mr. Hunter is a really nice man."

"I can be nice to Mr. Hunter and still go with Daddy when he comes for me," Melinda replied.

"That's true," Ainsley said even though she wanted to protest and tell Melinda her father wasn't coming for her. "And I would appreciate you being nice to Mr. Hunter."

"Can we go for ice cream tomorrow night after the pizza?" Melinda said hopefully.

Ainsley laughed. "Girl, you're pushing your luck with all this ice cream." Melinda grinned at her and licked at the cone she held in her hand.

Both mother and daughter were in good moods as they returned to their apartment. As they stepped out of the car, darkness had begun to fall.

Despite the shadows by the door, the square package on the stoop was hard to miss. Wrapped in bright pink paper and sporting pink and yellow ribbons, it looked like a birthday present waiting to be opened.

"Mom, is it your birthday?" Melinda immediately asked.

"No, honey. It isn't my birthday." Ainsley stared at the box, her heart thudding loudly in her ears. She knew Hunter was on patrol tonight, but there was no way he'd drop a package outside her door and not tell her about it. So, who had left it? And what was inside?

"It looks so pretty. Aren't you going to pick it up?" Melinda's voice reached through Ainsley's racing thoughts.

Ainsley bent over and picked it up and then unlocked the door and together they stepped into the little apartment. Ainsley carried the "present" into the kitchen and set it on the table.

She stared at it, unsure if she should be afraid or not. With the roses and the note, she had no idea what to expect. She suddenly became aware of Melinda staring at her curiously. "Mommy, aren't you going to open it?"

"Maybe later. Right now you need to go get ready for bed. You have school tomorrow."

Melinda looked at her curiously. "So, you aren't going to open it now?"

"No, honey. I might even wait and open it tomorrow night when Hunter gets here," Ainsley replied. "Now, run in and get a quick shower."

An hour later Melinda was in bed, and Ainsley sat at her table and eyed the package. She hadn't wanted to open it in front of Melinda in case it was something inappropriate for a young girl to see.

Just because the packaging was fun and pretty didn't mean there was something fun and pretty inside. Or did it? Dammit, who had left it for her?

There was no way she was going to wait until the next night to find out what was inside. She picked the present up and shook it. It had a little weight to it, but made no noise when she moved it back and forth.

Just open it, she told herself. Whatever was inside couldn't hurt her. She was being completely childish in being afraid of what she didn't know.

The present had obviously been wrapped with care. The ends were perfectly folded and taped. She opened one side. Beneath the wrapping paper was an ordinary brown cardboard box. Carefully she took off all the paper and folded it neatly.

She then eyed the cardboard box. She thought of the beautiful roses she'd received and then the nasty note. There was absolutely no way to anticipate what might be inside the package.

Just open the damned thing, she repeated to herself. She grabbed a pair of scissors, cut the tape across the top of the box and then opened the flaps.

A scream rose up inside her, and she slapped her hand over her mouth to keep it inside. She shoved away from the table, nausea threatening as fear and horror shot through her.

Hunter. She needed him. She leaned forward to grab her purse straps and then pulled it into her lap. She fumbled for her phone and then hit the button that would call him.

Chapter Nine

Hunter raced across town to get to Ainsley's place. Her tearful call had been nearly incoherent. All he really got out of it was that something had happened and she needed him.

Because there were few people out on the streets, he could push the speed limit to get to her. Unfortunately, he'd been on the other side of town when he'd gotten her call.

He wasn't supposed to be on duty at all, but he had taken on an extra shift because of another officer being off for a family death. With so few deputies in the town, it wasn't uncommon for all of them to pick up extra shifts to make sure the town was protected at all times.

He finally pulled up by her door. He'd barely gotten out of his car when she flew out of the apartment and into his arms. She cried into the front of his shirt, her body shaking as he pulled her close.

He let her cry for several moments and then he unwrapped her arms from around him. "Ainsley...honey, what's going on? What's happened?"

"I...we went to Melinda's a-appointment and then g-got ice cream and wh-when we got home there was a p-present on the doorstep." The words jerked out of her amid her tears.

"A present?"

She nodded and drew in several deep, long breaths in an obvious attempt to calm down. "It was wrapped up pretty like a present."

"Why don't we go inside so I can see it," he suggested.

"Melinda is asleep. I wanted to scream, Hunter." She grabbed his arm. "I still feel like screaming."

"You try not to scream and I'll try to keep it down so neither of us wake up your daughter," he said gently. He wrapped an arm around her shoulders and led her toward the door.

"It's on the kitchen table," she said. "I...I'm not sure what it is. All I saw was blood and fur." A sob choked out of her.

He went directly to the table where a square cardboard box set next to some ribbon and pink wrapping paper. She stopped behind him.

He opened the flaps and almost jumped backward. He forced himself to lean in to get a good look at what was inside. He grabbed gloves out of his back pocket and pulled them on, then moved the contents inside the box to better identify what it was.

"It's a dead rat," he said softly. It was a dead, bloody

rat with the throat cut. He closed the box and retaped the lid. "Do you have some sort of a sack I can carry all this out in?"

She went to the cabinet beneath the sink and pulled out a café takeout sack. "Hunter, please help me make sense of this," she said, her voice shaking as she handed him the sack.

"There is no sense to make of it," he replied tersely. Dammit, who was doing this to her? And why? A dead rat to him implied a threat even though no note was included. He quickly placed the box and the wrapping paper into the sack and then carried it out into the living room and set it just outside her door on the stoop.

He turned back to find her looking at him. She looked so small, so achingly vulnerable clad only in a pink nightshirt. Her eyes were filled with fear, and as she reached up to tuck a strand of hair behind her ear, her fingers trembled.

He took her hand in his and pulled her down to the sofa. He sank down next to her. Even though he was on duty, there was no way he could just walk away and leave her so frightened.

What he wanted to do was take her to bed and warm her body with his. He wanted to hold her through the night if that was as long as it took to make her fear ease.

"Ainsley, I swear I'm going to do everything in my power to get to the bottom of all this." He took her hand in his, hating how cold and small it felt in his.

"I just can't imagine why this is happening to me.

I've been nice to everyone I've met. I haven't caused any trouble for anyone." She held his gaze, and her eyes were filled not only with fear, but also confusion.

"I'm just as confused by all this as you are," he admitted. "But the good thing is nobody has tried to physically harm you."

"Not yet," she said darkly.

"I'm going to find this creep, Ainsley. It's possible I'll be able to pull some fingerprints off the wrapping paper or the box itself."

"I hope you can." She released a deep sigh. "I just want this all to end. I don't know who is doing this to me or why, but I want it to stop."

"I'm going to figure this out, Ainsley." He felt like he was saying the same words to her over and over again. "But in the meantime, if you get anything else like this, don't touch it and call me immediately."

"Trust me, I'll call you," she replied.

Reluctantly he released her hand. "I wish I could stay here with you, but I've got to get back to work. I'll make an official report on this, and I'm going to start interrogating people to see if somebody might know what this is all about."

She stood as he did, and she walked with him to the door. He pulled her into his arms and held her for several minutes. The trembling in her body finally ceased and reluctantly he released her.

"Ainsley, try not to worry. I won't let anything happen to you or your daughter. This is somebody who must just like the idea of freaking you out. Don't let them win."

"I'm trying not to be freaked out, but I am," she admitted.

"I know. Now, try to get a good night's sleep, and I'll talk to you tomorrow." He leaned forward and gave her a kiss on her forehead.

Minutes later he was back in his patrol car, seething with anger and hoping like hell the culprit had left a few fingerprints behind on the package.

Right now about the only thing he could arrest the perp for was trespassing. If he couldn't get the person in jail, then he'd make sure the person knew that to bother Ainsley again meant he was risking his health and well-being.

As he thought about Ainsley's fear, it ticked him off enough to want to beat the hell out of somebody. He now clenched his hands on the steering wheel.

Dammit, he didn't know whom to question. He'd never heard anyone speak negatively about her, so who was behind this reign of terror? He certainly didn't believe Ben Wilkins was capable of carrying out this kind of harassment.

A dead rat with its throat cut. Who was holding that kind of madness inside them? Who would think about catching a rat, slitting its throat and then packaging it up in pretty paper? It was such a disgusting and heinous thing to do.

He thought he knew the people of this small town. He knew the people who suffered from various mental issues and the ones who liked to cause trouble. But none of the people he knew had a mind so wicked as to do this to a vulnerable single woman.

He drove directly to the sheriff's station, eager to give the wrapping paper and box to fellow deputy Larry Knight, who was an expert at lifting fingerprints, among other lab-related things.

Unfortunately, Larry wasn't at work right now. Hunter called him and told him where to locate the items the next day when Larry came on duty.

Once that was finished, Hunter hit the road again. The first place he drove was to Lana Kincaid's house. The woman had worked as a waitress at the café for as long as Hunter could remember.

Lana knew practically everyone in town, and because gossip was rampant in the café she was the keeper of many secrets. She also probably knew more about the people in Dusty Gulch than he did.

She lived in a small ranch house on three acres just outside the main district. As he pulled in, lights shone out of her windows, letting him know she was still awake.

He parked and got out of his car. The front door opened just before he reached it, and Lana greeted him with a look of surprise. "Well, it's not often one of Dusty Gulch's finest comes visiting. Come on in." She opened the door to allow him entry.

He'd never been inside Lana's place before. He stepped into the living room and was vaguely surprised to see a pink zebra-striped sofa and a purple zebra-striped chair. The end tables and coffee table were glass, and the lamps on the end tables held enough sparkly crystals to blind a man.

Lana laughed. "It's all pretty unique, right?" She laughed and gestured him toward the sofa. "I bought all this stuff online after my last divorce. I know I don't have much decorating sense, but I just bought what I loved. I don't give a damn what other people think. If my next husband doesn't like my furniture, then he can stay in my garage. Now, can I get you something to drink?"

"No, thanks, I'm good. I just want to ask you a few questions." He sank down on the edge of the sofa.

She sat in the purple zebra chair, the light from the garish lamp glittering on the side of her face. "Questions about what?"

"About Ainsley."

"Has something else happened since she got that terrible note?" Lana leaned forward, obvious concern on her wrinkled face.

"Somebody delivered a rat with its throat cut to her doorstep this evening. It was wrapped up like a present."

"Oh my goodness. Who on earth would do such a thing?" she asked.

"I was hoping you could help me answer that," he replied.

"I can't imagine. Everyone at the café loves her. Not only is she gorgeous, but she's also a hard worker and very pleasant to be around."

"So, you haven't heard anyone speak ill about her?"

"Nobody." Lana laughed. "Hell, all the men want to date her and all the women want to be her." She sobered. "Honestly, Hunter, other than the skirmish she had with that drunk Ben Wilkins, she hasn't had any trouble with anyone."

"Do you know anyone who might be capable of doing these kinds of things to a vulnerable woman? Be honest, Lana. You've been around this town for a long time."

"I have, but I swear I don't know who is capable of this kind of crap. Slitting a rat's throat? That takes a particular kind of sick mind." Lana shook her head. "Is she in danger?"

"Let's hope not," Hunter replied even as a burn of anxiety lit his stomach on fire. He got up, and Lana walked with him to her door.

"I wish I could have been helpful, but honestly I've never heard anyone say a bad word about Ainsley. I care about that girl. I think she's a real sweetheart."

"Yeah, I kind of like her myself," Hunter replied with a small smile.

"I'll keep my ears to the ground for you," Lana said.

"I appreciate it, Lana."

As he drove away from Lana's place, her words echoed in his head. All the men wanted to date Ainsley, and all the women wanted to be her.

He'd just assumed the perp he was looking for was a man. But Lana's words made him wonder if it was possible it was a woman behind everything that was happening to Ainsley?

Maybe somebody who was jealous that she was gorgeous and friendly and had stirred up all the single men in town? God, it was bad to think there was a man who could do these horrible things, but somehow it was even worse to believe it was a woman.

EARLY THURSDAY MORNING Ainsley and her daughter went into the café for breakfast. While they ate she became aware of Big Ed sounding angry as he called out orders.

"What's up with the boss?" she asked Lana when she stopped to top off Ainsley's coffee.

"Ted didn't show up last night to do the cleaning," Lana said.

"That's a first. He's always been so reliable," Ainsley replied.

"Ed called his house this morning, and his wife said he'd left to meet a friend after dinner last night and she'd just assumed he'd gone ahead and come in to work after that. When she woke up this morning and he wasn't home, I guess she called the sheriff."

Ainsley shook her head. "I wonder what happened to him."

"Hopefully, Sheriff Black will be able to figure it out," Lana replied.

Ainsley found herself thinking about the missing janitor once Melinda had left for school and Ainsley was back in her apartment.

Even though she hadn't had much contact with him, she'd always found Ted to be an affable man. She hoped nothing bad had happened to him. However, even her concern about Ted couldn't halt the simmer of fear that had been her companion for what felt like forever.

Last night after Hunter had left, taking the horrendous "present" with him, she'd remained awake long into the night. There was no window in Melinda's room, but there was one in the kitchen and one in Ainsley's bedroom.

She'd spent half the night going back and forth between the two windows, peering out to see if anyone was lurking outside in the shadows of night. She saw nobody, but even when she got into bed, sleep continued to elude her.

She found herself going over everyone she had spoken to, all the people she had served since the moment she had landed in town and started working as a waitress.

There had to be somebody she had offended, somebody who now felt the right to torment and frighten her. Despite her need to identify somebody, she couldn't.

She hadn't spoken to Hunter yet today, although she knew they were still on to get pizza that evening. He'd been so sure in asserting to her that he was going to get to the bottom of this madness. But even though she believed he was a great deputy, he was only human, and if there were no clues to follow then how could anybody find the person responsible?

She tried to empty all that from her mind as she cleaned the apartment. Once she'd finished with her chores, it was just after noon. She made herself a tuna sandwich for lunch and then sank down on the sofa and tried to read a book.

No matter how hard she tried to concentrate on the words on the page, her thoughts kept going back to the dead rat that had been delivered to her doorstep.

What did it mean? Was it a warning to her? A warning about what? Aside from the horror of getting something like that was the confusion of wondering what, exactly, it meant in the long run?

Hunter called at two to make sure the plans for the evening were still a go. He also told her that they'd been able to pull fingerprints that they believed to be hers but had been unable to find any others.

Whoever the creep was, apparently he was smart enough not to leave a clue to his identity behind. Who in the heck was it? Her head hurt from trying to figure it all out.

By the time Melinda got home from school, Ainsley had her happy face on. The last thing she wanted was for Melinda to know things were happening that frightened her mother.

"Are you ready to go out with Hunter for pizza?" she asked her daughter. Melinda looked so sweet in a blue sweater that matched the pretty blue of her eyes and a pair of jeans. Her hair was in pigtails with blue ribbons streaming down the lengths.

"Sure." Melinda sank down on the sofa and smiled at her mother. "And I promise I'll behave."

"That's nice. I'm hoping you'll get to know Hunter better, because he's somebody important in my life and I'd like to think that he might become somebody important in your life."

"Like a stepdaddy," Melinda said. "Lisa at school has a stepdaddy and she likes him okay, but she still loves her real daddy."

"And you can still love your real dad," Ainsley said.

The conversation then turned to everything that had happened at school that day. They were still seated on the sofa when Hunter arrived for their evening out.

"Are you two ready for some pizza?" he asked. "Melinda…cheese pizza, right?"

"Right," she replied. "And I promised I'd be nicer to you tonight."

"I appreciate that." He smiled at Melinda.

Ainsley was grateful that he was keeping things light, although when he looked at her she saw his concern for her in the depths of his eyes.

Minutes later they were in his truck and headed to the pizza place. "I had to chase Ben Wilkins away from the café dumpster," he said softly.

She looked at him in surprise. "What was he doing back there?" Had she been wrong about Ben? Was it possible the drunk was behind all the things that had been going on?

"He was drunk and dumpster diving for food. He told me the café threw out better food than they sold.

Apparently whenever he gets hungry he goes to the dumpster."

"Do you think that was all he was doing there?" she asked.

"Yeah, I do. I honestly don't think Ben is the person we're looking for." He looked in the rearview mirror and smiled. "How are you doing back there, Melinda?"

"I'm good," she replied.

Ainsley just hoped Melinda stayed good for the duration of the date night. "I heard about Ted going missing. Did you all manage to find him today?" she asked Hunter.

He grimaced and shook his head. "No. We aren't even sure who he was meeting before going into work last night. His wife had no clue, and so far Ted is still missing. I feel like lately law enforcement is striking out all over the place."

"Hopefully, Ted will show up safe and sound," she said.

"And we'll figure out what's going on with you. That would be a big win-win."

He pulled up in front of the pizza parlor, and they all got out. They went inside and settled in one of the empty booths. Melinda sat next to her mother, and they both faced Hunter.

Facing him, Ainsley once again noticed what a handsome man he was. He could probably have his pick of any of the single women in Dusty Gulch, but he'd chosen her.

It just made the pressure to tell him the truth about

herself all the harder to bear. She'd decided she would wait until they figured out who was behind the things that had been happening to her. Once they had that answer, then she would come clean to him about her past. She only prayed he would understand and forgive her for lying to him.

They ordered their pizza, and while they waited the conversation was light and easy. She was pleased by how easily Hunter included Melinda, asking her questions in an obvious effort to get to know her better.

The pizza arrived, and Melinda remained on her best behavior. Hunter even managed to make her giggle several times. They finished their meal and then got back into Hunter's vehicle.

"I'm feeling like a little ice cream for dessert," he said as he started the engine. "Does anyone else in this car like ice cream as much as me?"

"I do," Melinda replied eagerly.

"Not me. I'm way too full of pizza to eat ice cream," Ainsley said.

Hunter laughed. "There's always room for ice cream, right, Melinda?"

"Right. Mr. Hunter, we could still go to the ice cream parlor and Mom doesn't have to get anything but you and I could get something."

"That sounds like a good plan to me," he replied. For the next five minutes, he and Melinda argued good-naturedly about what was the best kind of ice cream.

As Ainsley listened to the two of them—the two

most important people in her world—laugh and tease each other, a sense of rightness swept through her.

This was what she wanted for her future. The man she'd escaped had been a monster...a nightmare, but Hunter was her dream man and she could only hope that when everything was said and done, they would share a bright and future together.

"WHAT'S IN THAT bedroom where you spend so much of your time?" Sheila asked Peter.

The two of them were in the living room. He was in a chair and she was half sprawled on the sofa, on her way to drinking herself into oblivion. She held a tall glass of gin in her hand, and her voice was already slurred.

Pig, Peter thought to himself. She was a waste of air and space and he was sick of her. But he still needed her here. "It's my work," Peter replied and forced a smile to his face. "It's what keeps you enjoying all the goodies that you like."

She laughed and raised the glass to her lips. "I do like my goodies."

"Maybe it's time you call it a night," he suggested. The last thing he wanted to do was sit and talk to the woman. He'd much rather be alone with his thoughts of Colette.

"Just let me finish this glass," Sheila said and took another deep swallow.

Peter waited patiently. Once she'd drained the glass, she was toasted. He helped her to the bedroom, where she collapsed on the bed and within minutes was snoring.

Peter returned to the living room and his chair. It had been a good week. Twice he'd sat in the café eating while Colette had been serving tables on the other side of the room. She'd even looked at him several times, but no recognition had widened her eyes.

Then watching her reaction when she'd opened the present he'd left for her had been priceless. Her fear, her utter horror, had fed his very soul.

But he was tiring of the games. He'd already taken care of one loose end. It had been pathetically easy for him to lure Ted Johnson out here with the promise of more money. Ted had arrived and Peter had invited him into the kitchen. Thankfully, Sheila had been in one of her dope-enhanced nod outs and had no clue that they'd had a visitor.

He and Ted had shared a few drinks, and then when good old Ted was feeling nice and mellow, Peter had stabbed him. He'd slid the big, sharp knife in just under Ted's armpit and then had ripped it downward.

"Wha…" The single syllable had fallen from Ted's lips, and his eyes had widened. Before the man could say anything more, Peter carried him out to the porch and threw him into the pigpen.

It was true. Pigs could dispose of a human body in a very short time. He'd stood on his porch and listened to the pigs' frenzy. They squealed and fought each other to get a piece of the meat, and the sound of bones crunching filled the air.

When it was all over, there was nothing much left of Ted. Peter had then driven Ted's truck to an old shed on the property and parked it inside. And that was the end of Ted.

He was ready for his ultimate revenge. He was ready to make Colette learn the price for leaving him and shattering his world.

By listening in on her, he'd heard her make plans to go out with some girlfriends tomorrow night. Melinda was spending the night with a friend, and Deputy Do-Right was working. It would be a perfect night for a reunion.

And the pigs were still hungry.

Chapter Ten

Although Ainsley would much rather be spending her Friday evening with Hunter, he had to work, and so when Lana had approached her about several of the waitresses going out for drinks and to chill out, Ainsley had agreed to go with them.

Melinda had already made plans to spend the night with Bonnie, and in truth a little downtime with friends sounded good. It fact, it sounded wonderful. She hoped for just a little while she'd be able to get out of her own head and leave all the drama that had become her life at home.

Thursday night pizza had been a huge success. She believed real strides had been made between Hunter and Melinda. At the end of the night there had been no new "present" waiting for her, making the evening a real success in her book.

She now stood in her bathroom, putting on her makeup for the evening out. She had noticed there were two bars in the small town. The one on the edge of town, the Wrecking Ball, was supposed to be a nasty dive.

The other one, just off Main Street, was called Barney's Place and was supposed to be a nice place to get a drink, relax or do a little moving on the dance floor. Ainsley certainly didn't intend to do any dancing unless it was with Hunter, and since he wasn't going to be there, she'd be cooling her heels in a booth and visiting with Lana and the two other waitresses who were going.

She didn't intend to make it a late night. She had to open the café as usual the next morning, and she knew Lana wouldn't want a late night, either. They were all supposed to meet at eight, and she figured she'd probably be home by around ten.

At seven forty-five she walked out of her apartment and headed to her car. Already the shadows of night were beginning to fall. As she got inside her vehicle, she looked at the dumpster, but thankfully she didn't see anyone lurking around.

It was sad to think that Ben Wilkins lived on food out of the dumpster. Apparently he had nobody in his life who cared for him. He needed help, but there was nothing Ainsley could do about it.

Barney's Place was a fairly large bar with plenty of parking in front. Already the parking lot was filled with pickup trucks and cars, indicating that the bar was a popular place on a Friday night.

She scanned the area for Lana's car. The two had agreed to meet in the parking lot and enter the bar together. She finally spied her friend's car and pulled into the parking space next to it.

Lana got out of her car, looking like a woman on a mission to find her next husband—her purple pants hugged her legs, and her purple-and-white blouse displayed her full breasts.

"Wow," Ainsley said when she got out of her car. "You look hot."

Lana laughed. "I might be old, but I'm not dead."

"Have you seen Betsey and Abby yet?" Ainsley asked. The two women worked the same shifts as Ainsley and Lana.

"They came together about ten minutes ago. I told them to go on in and get us a booth or a table," Lana replied. "Let's head inside and find them."

Ainsley had never been in the bar before, and as they walked into the dim interior her nose was assailed by the odors of bar food, beer and various colognes and perfumes battling for dominance.

There was a long counter where people either sat on the stools or leaned in to order drinks. Booths were against both walls, and tables and chairs surrounded a decent-size dance floor. A live band was on a small stage just off the dance floor, playing a rousing country music song.

They found their friends in one of the booths, both with drinks already in front of them. "Hey, ladies," Betsey said in greeting.

Ainsley slid in next to Betsey, and Lana sat across from her and next to Abby. Almost as soon as they were seated, a waitress appeared to take Lana and Ainsley's orders.

Lana ordered a beer and Ainsley ordered a margarita, and within minutes the drinks were before them as the four chattered about work-related events from over the past week.

"I still can't believe Ted is missing," Betsey said. She twirled a strand of her long blond hair as her blue eyes widened. "I mean, it's like a real mystery."

"Yeah, he just seemed to vanish into thin air," Abby said. Abby was a favorite among the café diners. She was a short, cute redhead who always wore a smile. "Has Hunter told you anything about it?"

"No, we don't generally talk about his work," Ainsley replied.

"You've got your own mysteries going on," Lana said to Ainsley.

"I don't even want to think about all that tonight," Ainsley replied. "Tonight I'm on a mental vacation and all I want to do is relax and not think too much."

"Then we won't bring any of that up tonight," Lana assured her. "Tonight is for fun. We'll all worry about real-life stuff tomorrow."

Ainsley raised her glass. "I'll drink to that."

"Hell, I'll drink to anything," Lana said, making the others laugh.

For the next couple of hours, the women laughed and joked with each other. Lana saw several male friends in the crowd and occasionally got up to grab one and hit the dance floor.

Betsey also got up to dance while Abby and Ainsley remained seated. Abby had a serious boyfriend and, like Ainsley, had no intention of dancing with another man.

None of the women ordered a second drink. They were all responsible women who knew the dangers of driving while under the influence, and all four of them were working early the next morning.

However, that didn't stop them from having fun. Abby did impressions of some of their customers, and the other three practically rolled on the floor with laughter. After all the tension of the past couple of weeks, Ainsley was grateful for the lighthearted fun.

"Hey, Ainsley." Jimmy Miller appeared by the side of their booth. "I've never seen you in here before."

"That's because I've never been in here before," Ainsley replied.

He gestured toward the dance floor. "Why don't you come out with me and let me show you my smooth moves?"

"Sorry, Jimmy. I'm not here to dance. I'm just enjoying some time with my friends," she replied.

"I could be your friend," he returned.

"Buzz off, Jimmy. She's your friend, but her heart belongs to Hunter," Lana said. "And she only dances with her man. But I'll dance with you."

Jimmy backed up, a wide grin on his face. "Oh no, Lana, you know you scare the hell out of me." As he hurried away from the booth, they all laughed.

"I think that's my signal to call it a night," Ainsley said. It was already a few minutes after ten.

"Yeah, me too," Lana said. "As much as I hate to admit it, I can't stay up until all hours of the night and then work the early-morning shift the next day."

"At least we get a day off on Sunday," Ainsley said.

"I think Betsey and I are going to hang out here for just a little bit longer," Abby said.

"Then we'll see you two in the morning," Ainsley said.

They said their goodbyes, and then Ainsley and Lana left the bar together. They stepped out into the darkness and headed toward their cars.

"This was fun, and I needed to have a little fun and relaxation," Ainsley said.

"It was fun," Lana agreed. "It's nice that all of us get along so well."

"Abby and Betsey are so nice it would be hard not to get along with them," Ainsley replied.

"Isn't that the truth?" They reached the two cars. "Well, girlfriend, I guess I'll see you bright and early in the morning."

"Good night, Lana." Ainsley got into her car, grateful to turn on the heater as the night air was bordering on cold. She waited a couple of minutes for the car to warm up and then headed back to the apartment.

She was grateful that at least for the night she'd managed to put her worries away and really relax in a way she hadn't since she'd received the anonymous roses.

She stifled a yawn as she parked the car. Before she got out, she grabbed her cell phone. She'd promised she'd call Hunter when she got home.

"Hey," he said in greeting. "Did you have a good time?"

"I did. It was fun, but also very laid-back and relaxing," she replied. "And now I'm ready for a good night of sleep."

"I'm glad you had a good time. Are we still planning on the cookout at my place on Sunday?"

"We're up for it if you are." She looked toward the dumpster, grateful that once again she saw nothing and nobody to concern her.

"I can't wait to introduce Zeus to Melinda," he said.

She laughed. "I have a feeling it's going to be a match made in heaven."

"We'll see. In any case I'll come into the café tomorrow, so I'll see you then."

"Okay, good night, Hunter." Her smile still lingered on her lips as she finally left her car and went to the apartment door. She'd just put her key in the lock when, in her peripheral vision, she caught movement rushing toward her. She didn't even have a chance before she was slammed with her back against the door. Her breath whooshed out of her, momentarily rendering her helpless.

It was a man. He was clad all in black and wore a black ski mask. That's the only thing her brain could comprehend before his fist slammed her in the stomach.

Sharp pain weakened her knees, and nausea rose up inside her. Before she could recover, he tried to pick her up. Someplace in the back of her mind it registered that if he managed to pick her up and spirit her away, she'd never be seen again.

Sheer terror shuddered through her. She kicked and flailed her arms in an effort to keep him back. He punched out and connected with her jaw. Her head snapped back as a new pain roared through her and stars momentarily filled her head.

Tears blurred her vision as he continued to pummel her. She tried to kick him again. He grabbed her leg and pulled. She tumbled to the ground. She finally gained enough air to scream.

"Help," she cried. She screamed again. He kicked her in the ribs, and intense pain once again stole her breath away.

Who was it? Dear God, did he intend to beat her to death?

"What do you want?" she yelled with what breath she had left. "Help! Somebody please help me."

"Hey, leave her alone," a voice called out from the distance. "Hey, you…stop what you're doing. We need help over here."

"Help me," Ainsley screamed. The attacker kicked her in the ribs over and over again, making it impossible for her to scream or fight back. She curled up in a fetal ball in an effort to protect herself.

"Stop hurting her," the man cried out of the darkness. "I'm calling the police."

She managed to scream again, the other man continued to yell about getting the police and suddenly the attack stopped. She remained on the ground, sobbing and in so much pain she could hardly think.

"He's gone and I didn't really call the police because I don't have a phone." The words were slurred, and as he came closer to her she could smell the booze. "What can I do to help you?"

Ben Wilkins. Hysterical laughter rose up inside her. The town drunk…the man she had thrown out of the café…was her savior. The laughter quickly changed into deep sobs, and the sobs shot such excruciating pain through her ribs that darkness encroached and she knew no more.

"Boys, I KNOW THERE's marijuana in this car, because I can smell it." Hunter had just pulled over a car with four boys in it. They had blown through a red light on Main Street.

"I swear there's nothing in the car," the driver, Lenny Nicholas, said. "Maybe it's my cologne you smell."

Hunter laughed. "Right, and maybe you think I was born yesterday." He recognized all four of them—they weren't bad kids. "I know weed when I smell it. Now, do you want to hand it over to me? Or do you want me to call all your parents out here and then I'll conduct an official search of the car?"

They all protested until finally one of the boys in the back seat handed out a roach. "That's all we have left, Deputy Churchill. I swear. We just had one cigarette and we all took a puff off it and then we put it out," he said.

"Honestly, Deputy Churchill. That's the truth. The guys just wanted to try it," Lenny said. "I didn't have any. And that's all we have."

"You know I could arrest all of you. Weed is still illegal in this state, but I'm going to let you off with a warning tonight. Possessing weed is against the law, and smoking it doesn't make you cool. From now on I'm going to have my eyes on all of you."

"We didn't even like it," Lenny said. "That's why we didn't smoke the whole thing. It tastes nasty."

"I'm just warning you all. Next time I catch you with weed, it's going to be a whole different story. Now get out of here and don't run any more red lights."

As Hunter got back into his patrol car, Lenny eased away from the curb. Hunter placed the roach in a bag to be taken into the station and destroyed. He'd just pulled away when his phone rang.

He frowned as he saw Ainsley's number come up on the caller identification. What was she doing calling again? She should have been in bed and sound asleep by now.

He answered. "Ainsley?"

A male voice replied, his words a jumble Hunter couldn't understand. "Who is this?" he asked, a ring of alarm sounding in his head. Why would any male be on her phone?

"It's Ben. You know…Ben."

...d his main question continued to be who was be-...all this—who had attacked her with deadly intent ...ght? Hopefully Ben saw or heard something that ...ld help them identify the perpetrator. And hope-...y Nick and Zac would find some concrete evidence ...would lead to an arrest.

The Dusty Gulch Hospital was located in a large ...ck building that also housed several doctors' offices. ...nter parked and raced into the ambulance bay, but ...y had already unloaded her and taken her inside.

He walked around and entered into the emergency ...aiting room. Sandy Silver, a nurse he knew from ...round town, sat at a desk.

"Sandy, Ainsley Meadows just arrived in an am-...ulance. Could you tell the doctor on call that I'm out ...ere and need an update on her as soon as possible?"

"It's Dr. Lockwood tonight, and I'll let him know," ...e replied. She got up from the desk and disappeared ...rough a door that was marked No Entry.

Hunter started to sit in one of the green plastic ...airs, but he had far too much adrenaline rushing ...ough him to just sit. Instead while he waited, he ...ed the length of the small waiting room.

...andy returned. "He said he'd be out to speak with ...s soon as possible."

...hanks, Sandy." He resumed his pacing, but as the ...es ticked by, he finally sat and stared at the tile ...eneath his feet.

...he waited, he called Ed to let him know what ...ppened and told the man that Ainsley wouldn't

"Ben?" Hunter sat up straighter in his seat. What in the hell was going on? "Ben, where is Ainsley?"

The man began to sob, obviously drunk. "I can't wake her up."

"What do you mean, you can't wake her up?"

"She was…you know…attacked. A big man all in black hit her and kicked her. I wanted to call the po-lice, but I don't have a phone. I got into her purse to use her phone, but I didn't take nothing. I swear all I took out of her purse was her phone."

"Ben…where is she?" A sick horror filled Hunter. "Where are you, Ben?" he asked again urgently.

"I was dumpster diving. I know you told me not to, but I came back and I found a couple pieces of good meat, some fries and a whole loaf of bread."

"Dammit, Ben, are you at the café?"

"I thought I told you that," he replied.

Hunter hung up and turned his car around. He flipped on his siren and lights and drove as fast as possible. Blood rushed through his veins as an urgency he'd never felt before filled him.

Ben couldn't wake her…

She'd been attacked…

Ben couldn't wake her…couldn't wake her.

The words buzzed through his head over and over again. How badly was she hurt? Was she unconscious or was she… Oh God, his brain couldn't take him there.

He got on his radio and requested an ambulance to

meet him behind the café. He also radioed for more officers to meet him there.

She had to be all right. She just had to be. He continued to speed through the night to get to her, hoping and praying that she would be okay.

He pulled into the back of the café and turned his spotlight on. He immediately spied Ben half sprawled next to a prone, unmoving Ainsley in front of the apartment door.

He jumped out of his car and rushed to them. Ben looked up at him, drunken tears falling down his face. "She won't wake up. I should have done something sooner," he lamented. "I tried to help, but I'm nothing but a stupid drunk and the man scared the hell out of me."

Hunter crouched down, his heart thudding hard against his chest. He picked up one of her cold, lifeless hands and felt for a pulse.

His heart jumped into his throat as he waited to feel any stir of life. Was her heart no longer beating? There…he felt it. It was slow and faint, but it was there.

"I'm sorry," Ben half slobbered. "I should have done something more. I shouldn't have been so scared."

"Ben, move away. You did a great job and I appreciate you waiting here with her, but now I hear the ambulance coming," Hunter said. The ambulance couldn't get here fast enough for him. She needed immediate help.

Ben scooted back, and Hunter stared down at Ainsley. He didn't see any blood anywhere, but he did see

a blossoming bruise underneath her c[...] made his blood boil. Who had done th[...] what other injuries had she sustained?

Thankfully at that time the ambulan[...] and two of the paramedics jumped out of [...] grabbed a gurney. "I'm not sure what in[...] sustained, but she's been unconscious sin[...] on scene," Hunter told Matt Daniels, one o[...] medics.

Nick also showed up, along with Zac [...] other deputy working the late shift. As the p[...] ics loaded Ainsley onto the gurney and took of[...] hospital, Hunter turned to quickly explain the si[...] to the two deputies.

"Take Ben's statement, see if you can find ar[...] dence around the area and I'll be in touch. Rig[...] I'm heading to the hospital," he said.

"Don't worry, we'll take care of things her[...] assured him.

Hunter got back in his car and headed f[...] pital, his thoughts consumed with Ainsley'[...] Was she going to be all right? What had [...] before falling unconscious? The thought [...] beating her…the thought of her in pain [...]

Dammit. He clenched his hand arou[...] wheel as anger burned in his gut. It w[...] only directed at the perpetrator, but [...]

He should have seen something [...] When she'd received the dead rat, [...] ognized the situation had escalat[...]

be in to work for a while. He also asked if it would be okay for Melinda to spend the next day at his house. Ed assured him that it was fine, and Hunter promised to call him the next day.

He hoped Ainsley didn't get angry for him overstepping his boundaries, but he was relatively certain she would not be working and it was important to let Ed know as soon as possible so he could make the necessary adjustments.

When he'd hung up, his thoughts were as scattered as the stars in the sky. There were so many questions and no answers. Fear battled with anger as he waited to find out Ainsley's condition.

The outside door opened, and he looked up to see Sheriff Black walk in. "Wayne." Hunter stood.

"I got here as soon as I heard. How is she?"

The two men sat down side by side. "I haven't heard anything yet," Hunter replied. "She was unconscious when they brought her in, and it looked like she'd taken a punch to her jaw, but I don't know anything else yet."

"Well, I just wanted to come by and let you know I called in a couple more deputies to search the area around the café," Wayne said.

"Thanks, I appreciate it." Hunter raked a hand through his hair. "I don't have a clue who is behind this, but I'm sure it's the same person that left the nasty note in the café and a dead rat on her doorstep. Unfortunately, whoever it is, he's smart and hasn't left any clues behind."

"Hopefully that will change tonight and the men

will find something that will help identify the perp," Wayne replied. "In fact I'm on my way over there now." Wayne rose. "Let me know how Ainsley is doing. I'm putting Nick in charge of this investigation."

Hunter looked at him in surprise. "What? Why not me?"

"Hunter, you know there can't be any appearance of bias. You have a personal relationship with the victim, and that means you're off this case."

Hunter wanted to protest, but he knew Wayne was right, and the last thing Hunter wanted to do was give the perp a reason to have a defense due to bias on his part. "At least I know Nick will do a good job," he finally said.

He looked at the door where the doctor should come through. What was taking so long? His nerves jangled. How badly was she hurt?

"I'm off," Wayne said. "I expect to hear from you later, and I'm sure Nick will be in touch."

About fifteen minutes after Wayne left, Dr. Andrew Lockwood walked into the waiting room. Hunter shot up out of his chair and approached the doctor. "How is she?"

"She's alert and we have her resting comfortably," Dr. Lockwood said. "She has a broken rib and bruising all along her rib cage. She also took a pretty good blow to her chin. None of the injuries are life-threatening, but we're going to keep her for the rest of the night and, barring no complications, she should be able to go home tomorrow."

"But she was unconscious. What caused that?" Hunter asked even as an intense shudder of relief swept through him. The relief was short-lived as he thought of what she must have gone through.

"Shock and pain, but again, she's resting comfortably now," he replied. "We've given her something for her pain."

"Can I see her?"

Dr. Lockwood frowned. "Only for a short visit. What she needs right now is rest. She's in room 106."

Hunter raced down the quiet hallway and turned into her room. He paused in the threshold, aching at the very sight of her.

Her eyes were closed and she looked as pale as the white sheets that surrounded her except for the bright purple of the bruise on her chin.

As he stared at the bruise, and thought again of the broken and bruised ribs, a deep rage filled him. Who had done this to her? She was so kind...so giving and yet somebody had put their hands on her.

Her eyes suddenly fluttered open. She held his gaze for a long moment, and then she began to weep. "Honey...don't cry." He hurried to her side. He drew up a chair, sank down and took her hand in his. "Please don't cry. It's only going to make you hurt."

"I'm trying not to," she said and drew in several shallow breaths in an obvious effort to contain her emotions.

"I'm so sorry. Ainsley, I'm so damned sorry I didn't

see something like this coming. I'm so damned sorry that I wasn't there to protect you."

"Neither one of us saw something like this coming."

"You want to tell me what happened?"

As she gave him a blow-by-blow account of events from the time they had hung up with each other to when she had come to consciousness in the ambulance, once again a deep sense of rage filled him.

"Did you recognize anything about him? Anything at all?"

"No, he was dressed all in black and wore a ski mask. The only thing I can tell you is it's definitely a he, and he's strong." Tears filled her eyes once again. "I was terrified that he was going to pick me up and carry me away and I would never see Melinda or you again."

"Thank God that didn't happen. Did he say anything to you?"

"No, not a thing."

"What about smell? Did you notice anything about the way he smelled?"

She looked at him in surprise. "I hadn't thought about it." She frowned and then winced, as if the facial gesture had hurt her. "Now that I do think about it, he smelled…funky."

"You mean like dirty?"

"No, it wasn't the smell of perspiration or dirty clothes—it was a strange, nasty scent that I've never smelled before, and I can't even describe it. I'm sorry."

"Don't apologize," he said.

"Ben saved me. If he hadn't been there and yelled

out, I would have either been beaten to death or kidnapped."

"Thank God for dumpster-diving drunks," he replied.

"Thank God," she echoed.

She closed her eyes for a long moment, and when she finally looked at him again, he saw not only exhaustion in her eyes, but also realized whatever they had given her for pain was making her sleepy.

"You get some rest now," he said and released his hold on her hand. He half rose up and then leaned over and kissed her softly on her forehead. "I'll be back tomorrow, okay?"

"Okay." She closed her eyes once again and appeared to be asleep before he even left her bedside.

He remained in her doorway for several long moments, his thoughts tortured by what had happened to Ainsley. He had to figure out a way to keep her safe. His gut clenched. He had to keep her safe, because he didn't believe this was the end of it. Somebody wanted her dead, and Hunter had a terrible feeling that the man wouldn't stop until he'd achieved his goal.

Chapter Eleven

Ainsley opened her eyes to the early-morning sun drifting into her hospital room. She instinctively knew that to move meant pain, and so she stayed still.

She vaguely remembered Hunter stopping by the night before. She'd felt his concern and caring, and it had almost warmed up all the iciness in her soul... almost, but not quite. And that iciness encased her heart once again this morning.

She was scared. No, she was absolutely terrified. Not only by what had happened the night before, but also about what might happen in the future.

If the man last night had wanted to kidnap her, he'd failed. If he'd wanted to kill her, he'd also failed at that, too. Would he try again? Was he out there now already planning his next attack on her?

And as always, her biggest question was who was it? Who had attacked her last night? She now positively knew Ben Wilkins had nothing to do with it. In fact, if he hadn't been dumpster diving again last night, she would probably be dead by now.

There was obviously something good and decent still left in Ben. He could have stayed hidden behind the dumpster while she was being attacked. But instead, even drunk, he'd done what he could to help her. He'd saved her life.

She tried to draw a deep breath, but pain ripped through her ribs where the man had kicked her. Her jaw ached, and overall she felt as if she'd gone ten rounds with a heavyweight boxing champion.

Finding the remote for her bed, she pressed the button to raise her head. She moaned as her body readjusted to the new position.

At that moment Callie Roberts walked in. "Oh good. You're awake," she said. "I'm just going to take your vitals." She prepared the blood pressure cuff. She plumped it up and then slowly released it.

After a minute or so, she pulled off the cuff and smiled at Ainsley. "A little high, but that's probably due to pain."

"Oh, I'm definitely in some pain," Ainsley replied, even as she tried to smile at the young nurse.

"The doctor ordered something to help with that. I'll be right back in with it."

As Ainsley waited, she thought of her daughter. Thank goodness she was at Juanita's. Once it got a little later in the day, she'd check in there.

An hour later Ainsley felt a little better. The medicine had taken the edge off her pain, and she drifted in and out of sleep.

She came awake again and was surprised to see Hunter sitting in the chair next to her bed.

"Hi," he said.

"Hi," she replied and forced a smile. "Fancy meeting you here."

"I'd rather be meeting you anywhere but here," he replied. His green eyes held such warmth, such caring it took away what breath she had. He reached for her hand and gave it a gentle squeeze. "How are you doing this morning?"

"I hurt, but I'm better than I was last night," she replied. "But I'm not going to lie…I'm scared, Hunter. I just know the man last night first tried to kidnap me, and when he couldn't get me up, he wanted to kill me."

"Nick has been assigned to the case. I haven't spoken to him this morning, but I'm hoping he got something to help us identify this guy."

"And if he doesn't?"

"Then we'll keep digging until we find him." His voice was filled with grim determination, but as much as she wanted to believe his words, in this case she felt like the bad guy was definitely winning.

"Thank God Melinda wasn't with me last night," she said. "But what happens next time?"

"There won't be a next time," he said firmly. "I don't want you and Melinda going back to your apartment. Until we find this guy, I want the two of you to move into my place."

She looked at him in stunned surprise, and then

more than a little bit of relief flooded through her. "Are you sure you want to do that?"

"Positive," he replied firmly. "According to the doctor, you're probably going to be released today. My plan is to get Melinda and we'll go to your place and you can pack up what you need."

"What about my work?"

"Ainsley, the last thing you need to worry about right now is your job. First of all, you need time to rest and heal. I already talked to Ed to let him know what's going on, and he knows you won't be working for a while." He squeezed her hand once again. "I don't want you to worry about anything."

She laughed and then winced. "Oh Hunter, right now I'm worried about everything."

"Well, stop it. My shoulders are broad, and you can leave the worry to me."

She studied his features without speaking for a long moment. He was so handsome and so earnest in this moment. "I wish it were that easy," she finally said.

"Me too," he replied.

At that moment Dr. Lockwood entered the room. "On a scale of one to ten, ten being the worst pain you've ever experienced, where are you right now?"

"Before the pain medicine, I would have said about an eight, but now I'd say I'm about a six," she replied.

He nodded. "The good news is I'm going to release you today, and I'm going to write a script for ten days of pain meds. The bad news is that these injuries are going to take some time to stop hurting."

"I figured that," she replied. She'd had broken ribs before and knew they took a long time to heal.

"I'll send the nurse in to remove your IV and will write up the paperwork to get you out of here."

An hour later Hunter helped her walk out of the hospital and to his truck. "I guess they didn't feed you any breakfast. You want to grab something in the café before we pick up Melinda?"

"That's not necessary. I'm really not hungry," she replied.

"Okay, then we'll go get your daughter and head to your place so the two of you can pack."

"Don't you have to work today?" she asked.

"I took the day off. At least when I have to go in to work tomorrow, I know you and Melinda will be safer at my place. My doors and locks are better than the ones in your apartment. I don't like the idea that not only could anyone come through your front door, but they could also come through the door that separates your apartment from the café."

"How are we going to do this? You only have one bedroom available," she said.

"You and Melinda will have the bedroom, and I'll bunk on the sofa."

"Oh Hunter, I don't want you to make that kind of a sacrifice for us," she protested.

"Nonsense, it's not a sacrifice at all. I can't tell you how many times I've fallen asleep on my sofa. It's really quite comfortable."

She smiled at him. "You'd tell me that even if your sofa was made of rocks."

He returned her smile. "Probably, but thankfully my sofa isn't made of rocks."

They fell silent for a few minutes as he drove to Ed and Juanita's house. A million thoughts burned through her head as she stared out the passenger window.

Surely she would be safer at Hunter's place than at her own. Hopefully the man who was after her wouldn't know where she'd gone. If Hunter kept his usual schedule and she and Melinda didn't peek outside, maybe nobody would even know they were there.

She almost laughed at her own stupidity. Of course everyone in town would know where she'd gone because everyone in town knew she and Hunter were a couple. Still, there was no question she'd feel safer staying there.

She'd have to keep Melinda out of school for a while, but that seemed a small price to pay for their safety. Or she could pack up their things and run.

God, the very thought of starting over someplace else broke her heart. Despite what was happening to her, she still loved it here in Dusty Gulch. She still believed in the goodness of most people here. This was exactly the place where she wanted to raise her daughter.

She certainly didn't want to give up Hunter and the life she saw here with him because of the actions of a single person. She would give this plan a chance and hope within the next couple of days her attacker would be arrested.

Fifteen minutes later they were seated at Juanita's kitchen table. "You know Ed won't be happy about losing one of his favorite waitresses for a while, but we both want you to take all the time you need to get the healing you need," she said.

"Thanks, Juanita. I couldn't do a good job for Ed right now no matter how much I wanted to," Ainsley replied.

"With that in mind, why don't you let Melinda stay here with us for a week or two? I can get her to school in the mornings, and you know she's always good for me."

"Oh no, that's asking too much," Ainsley protested.

"Nonsense. We'd love to have her. Let me take care of her while you take care of yourself," Juanita replied.

"Are you sure you wouldn't mind?" Ainsley felt the hot press of tears of gratitude. This was why she loved this town…because of people like Juanita and Ed. For all of Ed's blustering, he had a heart of gold.

"If I minded, I wouldn't have brought it up," Juanita replied. "My friend, please, let me do this for you."

Ainsley looked at Hunter and then back at Juanita. "Okay, but I'll need to take her home now so she can pick out some clothes to pack and then we'll bring her back here."

"I'll go get her." Juanita got up from the table and disappeared from the room.

"Are you okay with this?" Hunter asked her softly.

"Actually, I'm a little bit relieved. Melinda will stay in school and Juanita will keep her on a regular routine. I won't worry about her if she's here."

Melinda and Juanita's daughter Bonnie came running into the room. "Is it true, Mom? I get to stay here for a whole week or maybe more?"

"Would you like that?" Ainsley asked.

Melinda and Bonnie hugged each other and bounced up and down with excitement. "Yes, I would like it," Melinda exclaimed.

"Then you need to come with us right now so you can pack a bag and then we'll bring you back here," Ainsley said.

"Awesome," Melinda replied and then frowned. "What happened to your chin?"

"I…uh…I took a nasty fall last night. I hit my chin and hurt my ribs," Ainsley said. The last thing she wanted was for her daughter to be afraid.

Melinda's features softened, and she released her hold on Bonnie and sidled up next to Ainsley. "Do you want me to come home and take care of you?"

Ainsley wrapped an arm around her daughter. "No, honey. I'll be fine. I'm going to stay at Hunter's house while you stay here."

"Are you sure?" Melinda asked. "Will he take good care of you?"

"I promise I will," Hunter said.

Ainsley smiled. "Okay then, let's get going so we can get your clothes for a week."

Within minutes the three of them were headed back

to the apartment. When they arrived, Ainsley stared at the door, replaying what had happened the last time she'd stood at that door.

Icy chills raced up and down her spine, and her ribs hurt even more as she remembered the kicks she'd received. "Okay?" Hunter asked softly, as if he knew how hard it was for her to come back here.

She straightened her back and reached for the inner strength that had gotten her through hell in the past. "I'm fine," she replied. "Let's just get this done."

They entered the apartment, and Hunter headed for the sofa. "Melinda, get out your pink suitcase and pack it with school and play clothes. I'll be in to check it in just a few minutes," Ainsley said.

Hunter sat on the sofa while Ainsley went into her bedroom and Melinda went into hers. From the closet Ainsley pulled out a suitcase and opened it on the floor. There was no way with her screaming ribs she could lift it onto the bed.

She paused for a moment, trying to decide what she should take with her for being gone for a week or two. With her ribs hurting like they did, all she wanted was loose-fitting pants and T-shirts.

She quickly packed up what she thought she would need and grabbed her bag of toiletries off the back of the stool in the bathroom. Before going back to her room, she decided to check in on Melinda.

She was about to enter her daughter's bedroom when she heard it…the unmistakable deep voice of her ex-husband coming from someplace inside the room.

Shock and then a wild terror froze her in place. The toiletry bag fell from her hand, and a scream lodged in the back of her throat.

"I'm coming soon for you, baby girl," the disembodied voice said.

Peter...he was here.

Oh God, he'd found them again.

He was not only someplace in Dusty Gulch, he was in their apartment. She backed away from Melinda's bedroom, a scream begging to be released.

After all this time, when she was sure she was safe, she wasn't. He'd found her, and it was only a matter of time before he'd kill her.

HUNTER KNEW THE minute Ainsley came into the living room that something had happened. Her face was white, and her entire body was visibly trembling.

"Honey, what's wrong?" he asked. He jumped up off the sofa.

She motioned for him to step outside the door. When they stood on the stoop, she stared at him for a long moment. "I need to go. I really care about you, but I need to pack up everything in my car and get out of town as fast as I can," she whispered.

He frowned. "Ainsley, what are you talking about?"

"Melinda hasn't been lying. Her father has been talking to her. I heard him just now. Peter is here and I've got to leave town."

The words flew out of her in a rush. Hunter could

feel her desperate urgency, an urgency he didn't understand. "You heard him? What do you mean? Where?"

"Just now in Melinda's room." Her voice rose with
hysteria. "I've got to go."

What the hell was going on? "I thought your ex-
husband didn't care about you or Melinda."

"I lied, and now I've got to leave. I…I've got to take
Melinda and run." She whirled around to go back inside, but he caught her by the arm to stop her.

"Ainsley, listen to me. I don't know what's going
on right now, but we have a plan. Just get your things
to go to my place, and Melinda will be safe with Ed
and Juanita."

"You don't understand, but I need to run. It's…it's
what we do. I…I need to find a place where he can't
find us. He's going to take Melinda and he's going to…
to kill me." Her eyes were huge pools of abject terror
as she clutched at the front of his shirt.

"Ainsley, try to calm down. You don't have to run.
We now know who the bad guy is. We'll get him. We're
going to find him and get him behind bars. I just need
for you to give me some time and some more information. Can you do that, baby?" He took her by the
shoulders. "Can you trust me?"

She held his gaze for several long minutes, and he
could feel some of the sick energy inside her ease away.
"Okay, I'll try things your way for now."

"Let's go back inside." He pushed his car keys into
her hand. "Get you and Melinda packed up and leave

the suitcases in your rooms. Then go lock yourselves in my truck. Is there attic access in your apartment?"

Once again she clutched at the front of his shirt. "Don't go up there. He'll…he'll kill you, Hunter. He's a very sick, dangerous man."

Hunter touched the handle of his gun in his holster. "You don't understand. When somebody threatens somebody I love, I become a dangerous man. Now, where's the attic access?"

"In the bathroom," she finally said.

"Thank you." He leaned over and gave her a quick kiss on the forehead. "Get packed and get in the truck, okay? You have a flashlight?"

"Under the kitchen sink." Her fingers tightened on the front of his shirt. "Please, Hunter. Don't let him kill you."

"I won't," he replied firmly.

They went back inside, and within minutes Melinda and Ainsley were packed and locked inside the truck. The moment they left the apartment, Hunter grabbed the flashlight beneath her kitchen sink and then hurried into the bathroom.

He stepped up on the toilet lid and then onto the edge of the sink, where he had to crouch. He reached up to move the piece of ceiling that gave access to the attic. Once it was dislodged, he pulled his gun. He wasn't about to stand all the way up not knowing if he'd catch a bullet in the head.

"Dusty Gulch Sheriff's Department. Come down with your hands up." He waited and listened. Nothing.

He repeated the command and again waited to hear something…anything that would let him know where the man was in what he assumed was a very large attic.

Still he heard nothing. Not a rustle, not any movement that would indicate anyone in the immediate space.

His heart pounded fast and furiously. Adrenaline poured through his veins. He finally straightened up, leading the way with his gun and the flashlight.

He pointed the light to the left and then slowly panned to the right. He didn't see anyone. He stuck the light and his gun in his waistband and then pulled himself up and into the attic. He quickly grabbed the light and his gun once again.

Once again he scanned the area with his light. There didn't appear to be another person up here. Had the perp already escaped through another access?

He was about to take a couple of careful steps forward when he saw them…a tangle of wires that he knew didn't belong up there.

Realization struck him. Ainsley and her daughter had been spied on, and there had to be speakers involved so that the man could talk to his daughter. How long had these things been up here? Who in the hell was Ainsley's ex-husband?

He got down from the attic and went into Melinda's room. He spied the camera in the ceiling, along with a tiny little speaker, and he knew there were others located around the apartment.

He immediately called Nick. "Hey, man, I was

going to catch up with you and Ainsley later today. How's she doing?"

"She's sore, but doing okay. I'm moving her into my house right now. You need to get to the café and check out the attic above her rooms. There are cameras and I don't know what else up here to spy on her."

"What?" Nick's voice was filled with stunned surprise.

"Yeah, and we now know who the bad guy is. It's Ainsley's ex-husband. I'm hoping she has a picture of him on her phone or someplace so we can find him and get him in jail." Hunter spoke fast, aware of the two waiting in the car. "I'm leaving her apartment right now. We'll be at my place in just a little while."

"Okay, I'll head to the café right now and touch base with you later."

The two men hung up, and Hunter hurried into Melinda's room and grabbed her small, pink-flowered suitcase and then went into Ainsley's bedroom and picked up her black suitcase. He carried them outside and loaded them into the truck, then got behind the steering wheel with a reassuring smile at Ainsley.

She didn't smile back. She stared out the passenger window and her trembling fingers twisted into knots in her lap. Once they were alone, he had a lot of questions for her.

She'd already confessed she'd lied to him about her ex-husband. What else might she have lied about? He definitely needed some answers from her.

He also needed any information she had about her

ex-husband. If he was the person who had attacked her the night before, then he was in town and hopefully Nick and the other law enforcement officials could find him and get him in jail so that Ainsley and Melinda would be safe.

They took Melinda back to Juanita's, and during the ride to his house Ainsley remained silent and withdrawn. He was completely and totally in love with her. The utter depth of his love for her hit him out of left field.

He'd known he enjoyed spending time with her. He knew that he liked everything about her. He'd realized he'd been working toward a future with her. He'd told Nick he was thinking about proposing to her. He was definitely in love with her, but he wondered what kind of secrets she was keeping.

He'd been open and honest with her about everything in his life, and he'd believed she was open and honest with him. Now doubts twisted his gut. Why hadn't she told him her ex-husband was a dangerous man before now?

They arrived at his place, and he carried her suitcase through his front door. "Come on into the bedroom." He led her into the room and placed her suitcase next to the bed. "You can unpack later. Right now we need to talk."

She gave a curt nod and then followed him into the living room. She sat on the sofa, her arms wrapped around her middle. She looked so beautiful and yet so small and vulnerable.

He wanted to sit next to her and draw her into his arms. He wanted to tell her how much he loved her and that he wanted a forever future with her, but he didn't. He had more important things to do.

He got a small notebook and a pen from his kitchen desk drawer and then joined her on the sofa. "What's your ex-husband's name?"

"Peter Waverly." She didn't meet his gaze.

"Do you have a picture of him?" If they had a photo of him, then they could immediately show it around town. Somewhere somebody had to have seen the guy.

"In my phone," she replied. "It's in my purse in the bedroom. I'll go get it." She got up and left the living room.

This was the break they had needed. Why hadn't she told him more about this man before now? If she knew her ex was dangerous, then why hadn't she shared with him more about the man when inexplicable things had started to happen to her?

She came back in and resumed her position on the sofa next to him. She turned on her phone and flipped through a dozen photos and then stopped.

When she gave him the phone, her hand trembled. "He's going to kill me. He tried to kill me before."

Hunter looked at the photo. There was nothing distinctive about the man. His blond hair was cut short and his blue eyes stared straight into the camera. His front teeth overlapped each other, giving him a slightly crooked smile. Hunter didn't remember seeing the man anywhere around, but that didn't mean he wasn't here.

He grabbed his cell phone and once again called Nick. "I've got a picture of our perp. It's on Ainsley's cell phone. I'm going to send it to you right now," he said when Nick answered.

"I've got it," Nick said after a moment. "I'll get copies printed off and we'll get it circulating. Tell Ainsley we're going to get him behind bars."

"I'll tell her." Hunter hung up the phone and handed hers back to her. For several long moments, they sat in silence. So many questions whirled around in his head, he didn't even know where to begin.

"How long have you known it was your ex-husband behind everything?" he finally asked.

"When I heard his voice in Melinda's room. Before that I just assumed it was somebody here in town who was tormenting me." Her voice was a dull monotone. "I should have known he would find us. He's found us no matter where we've been. He won't stop until he kills me."

She raised her gaze and looked at him, and in the depths of her eyes he saw more secrets—dark secrets he feared might destroy everything they had built between them.

"Why does he want you dead?" he asked.

"Because I left him. I belonged to Peter and he's a narcissistic psychopath. He tried to kill me before I left him, and he's been hunting me ever since."

"So, he was abusive in the marriage?" Anger rose up inside him. He'd never been able to understand how a man could put his hands on a woman…especially a woman he professed to love.

"The physical abuse didn't really start until the last two years of our marriage. Before that there was definitely mental and emotional abuse."

She shook her head and once again looked down at her hands in her lap. "It's a typical story of domestic abuse. First he began to isolate me from my friends and family. I was rarely allowed to go anywhere on my own. I didn't have a car or a bank account."

She sighed, sounding impatient. "And then one day he thought I flirted with a stock boy in the grocery store. That night was the first time he beat the hell out of me. I should have left then, but he was so contrite afterward, and I was desperate to stay together for Melinda's sake."

"And then he kept beating you," he said. When he thought of what she'd apparently gone through, he wanted to find her ex and beat him to a bloody pulp.

"He did. When he beat me the last time, I was sure he was going to kill me. There was no car accident to make the scar on my stomach. He stabbed me there and would have stabbed me to death if the neighbors hadn't heard me screaming and called the police."

She released a sigh that sounded bone-weary. "He was arrested that night and I packed up what I could, used his bank card, which he'd left behind, to withdraw as much money as I could, and I took Melinda and we left."

"Why didn't you tell me all this before now?" He

felt lied to—granted, it was a lie by omission, but he didn't understand why she hadn't shared this with him before now.

"Oh, Hunter, I didn't want anyone to know where I'd come from. I have been so afraid for so long, and I've told you so many lies I don't even know where to begin to tell you the truth."

He stared at her. A woman's lies had destroyed his life before. He now had a dreadful sense of déjà vu. Was it about to happen all over again?

Chapter Twelve

Ainsley had been terrified since she'd heard Peter's voice in Melinda's room. She'd hoped Peter had given up on looking for her and moved on. She'd desperately hoped she and her daughter were finally free of him.

She should have known better. He was totally obsessed. He was a sick man who wanted her dead. She should have known when strange things had begun to happen to her that he was behind it all.

She felt Hunter's stare on her, and even though this wasn't the way she'd wanted to come clean to him, she owed him the whole, unvarnished truth.

He was going to hate her for her lies, and then if he did his job, he would have to place her under arrest. Dear God, how had it all come down to this?

"Peter came from money. His father was not only rich, but also influential. After I got medical treatment for the stab wounds I'd received, I took Melinda to a motel to wait to see what happened next."

"So, what happened next?"

There was curiosity in his voice, but she also felt a

touch of coolness from him. The dream she'd had of building a future with him was now shattered. As she looked at him and saw that his beautiful green eyes were guarded, she knew the truth. Peter had won. She felt as if she was already dead.

"Peter was out of jail the next morning with no charges levied against him. He'd tried to kill me and he walked away free as a bird."

"Was this in Nevada?" Hunter asked.

"No, I lied about being from Nevada. I'm actually from Portland, Maine. My mother lives there along with my older sister. My name isn't really Ainsley Meadows, it's Colette Waverly."

He winced, as if she'd physically slapped him. "So, he got no charges and you ran," he said flatly.

She nodded. "While I was running for my life, he divorced me and won full custody of Melinda. Apparently, he told the judge that I was dangerous and deranged. A warrant was issued for my arrest and I was charged with parental alienation, among other things. But there was no way I was going to allow my daughter to live with that madman, so for the past three years I've been on the run. I have fake ID and I've broken all kinds of laws to stay one step ahead of the monster. So, I understand if you have to arrest me."

The words burst out of her on a rush, and when there was nothing else left to say, she put her hands up to her face and began to weep.

She was utterly exhausted. Her body hurt from the beating she'd received the night before. Her heart ached with the distance she now felt from Hunter, with the damage she had done to their relationship.

All she could think about now was if he didn't arrest her, then she needed to get out of here and return to her life on the run. She would never, ever allow herself to get close to anyone again, but she couldn't take back the love she felt for Hunter.

She wished he would take her in his arms and tell her everything was going to be okay. She wanted to be in his embrace, where she'd always felt so loved and protected. She stopped crying and dropped her hands back into her lap.

"Are you going to arrest me?" she finally asked. She met his gaze once again.

"I'm betting that if I don't arrest you then you're going to take off again. Aren't you tired of running?" His eyes were dark, unfathomable.

"Yes," she replied as tears blurred her vision. "Oh God, I'm exhausted. I'm sick of the lying and the looking over my shoulder. I don't want this kind of life for Melinda. I know it's not good for her, but I didn't feel like I had any other options. I was really hoping this would be our forever home."

"Then stop running. Stay here and let us do our jobs. We'll deal with your other legal issues once we get Peter behind bars." A knock on the door interrupted whatever else he was going to say.

He got up to answer the door and returned a moment later with Nick. "Hey, Ainsley, how are you doing?" Nick asked her.

"Okay," she replied even though she was anything but okay. At the moment her physical pain was second to the pain that stabbed in her heart.

She wasn't sure what Hunter was going to do, but she was pretty sure any love he'd had for her was gone. Thoughts of that squeezed her heart so hard it made her ribs scream in pain.

"I just wanted to let the two of you know where we're at in the investigation." Nick sat in the chair facing the sofa, and Hunter eased back down beside Colette. "I've got men up in the attic at the café dealing with all the surveillance equipment." He looked at Hunter. "This guy spent a ton of money on this, and we have no idea where the location is on the other end. We also don't know how he managed to get everything up there."

"Maybe the person who has that answer is Ted Johnson, who's nowhere to be found."

"If he had anything to do with Peter, then he's probably dead," Colette said. If the man was dead, then she was partially responsible for his death. If she'd never come to Dusty Gulch, then Peter wouldn't have killed Ted. "Peter would consider Ted a loose end. I can't emphasize enough to you both what a dangerous, evil human being he is."

She fell silent as Hunter filled Nick in on her real name, the reasons for her lying to everyone in town and about her abusive life with her ex-husband.

Nick listened carefully to everything. "Thankfully we now have his picture being circulated by all the deputies in town. If he's here in town, then somebody will have seen him," Nick said. "It's just a matter of time before we have him arrested."

"I hope so," she replied. And then what? Peter would go to jail, and if it was like the last time, he'd manage to get out of it. He'd be out and she'd be arrested and he'd have full access to Melinda. He would discipline Melinda the same way he had her...with his fists and with his hurtful, damaging words. This thought once again brought tears to her eyes.

"Is there anything else you can tell us about Peter that might help us in locating him and making an arrest?" Nick asked her.

"Nothing. I could never predict what Peter might do," she replied tiredly. Had it only been hours ago that she'd left the hospital? It already felt like it had been months.

"Of course we all know it's possible he's changed his hair color or grown some facial hair," Nick said and then stood. "I'm heading back to the café to check in on the men there. Ainsley...er...Colette, I'll be in touch. Hunter...walk me out?"

She watched as the man she loved disappeared out the front door with Nick. She had found the town she'd wanted to be her forever home and the man she'd hoped would be her forever man. And now it had all been destroyed.

She never should have tried to be happy. When Hunter had first asked her out, she should have turned him down. She never should have allowed herself to care about or to be cared for by another human being.

Right now, even if she got the opportunity, she didn't have the strength to even think about running again. She felt utterly hopeless. If Peter didn't kill her this time, then he would just wait for the next opportunity he got.

She had little hope that they would find him. He was incredibly smart, and it was quite possible he'd already left town. He had to have known she'd heard his voice in the apartment. He had to have seen Hunter going up into the attic and known they would now be looking for him.

She wasn't afraid of dying. What she was afraid of was leaving Melinda in Peter's care. She would willingly give her own life if it would stop that from happening.

She looked up when Hunter returned. He stood in the doorway between the kitchen and the living room. "Why don't you get unpacked now and I'll see about making us something to eat?"

There was nothing warm or supportive in his eyes at the moment, and an exquisite pain of bereavement shot through her. Without saying a word, she got up and went into his bedroom to unpack some of her things.

Before she even got started, she sank down on the bed and was struck by a deep exhaustion. It was an exhaustion created by both mental and physical pain… one of utter despair.

Her body hurt, and at least she could help that. She

dug in her purse, grabbed one of her pain pills and dry swallowed it. Maybe she'd just rest for a few minutes before unloading her suitcase. She stretched out on the bed and was instantly enveloped by Hunter's scent.

She closed her eyes, breathing in the essence of him. It was a smell that had always signified love and protection. She began to cry quietly—from the pain, from the fear and finally for everything she had lost.

She drew in several deep breaths to staunch her tears. When she stopped weeping, her eyelids felt too heavy to lift. Her last conscious thought was that it was just a matter of time before all her nightmares where Peter was concerned came true and all her dreams of Hunter would shatter.

HUNTER THOUGHT MAYBE a bowl of soup with some crackers might taste good to her. He had both chicken noodle and tomato. Since he had no clue which one she might like, he pulled them both out of his pantry along with a box of saltines.

He then sat at the table to await her return. Her... not Ainsley, but Colette. He was still trying to wrap his head around everything he'd learned about her.

His thoughts were disjointed and his emotions were all over the place. Anger battled with disappointment and created an enormous sense of loss inside him.

If she'd lied to him about her name and where she was from, what else had she lied about? Had her kisses been a lie? When she told him that she cared about him, had that been a fabrication?

Had she gone out with him in the first place thinking that dating a deputy was smart given her circumstances? Was it a case of keeping her friends close and her enemies closer? Had she gone out with him simply because she thought he would keep her safe?

He couldn't figure out what was real and what wasn't where she—Colette, not Ainsley—was concerned.

She should have returned to the kitchen by now. She'd had plenty of time to unpack. A small bell of alarm rang in his head. He got up and walked through the living room and then paused and listened.

There was no sound coming from his bedroom. Had she opened a window and taken off? Had she decided that running was better than trusting him? He hurried down the hallway and stopped short in the doorway, relief flooding through him. She hadn't run—she'd fallen asleep.

She was on her back, her dark hair fanned out against his pillow. She looked beautiful in sleep. All the worry and stress lines were gone from her face.

It had all seemed so real with her. He'd really believed he'd tasted her desire for him in her kisses. When they'd made love, he'd truly believed she was falling in love with him.

Had it all been an act? Had she just been using him all along? He couldn't help but wonder what other secrets she might have, although the ones he'd already learned were devastating enough.

The doubts about her and her actions since coming

to town created a pool of deep disappointment and loss inside him. He was so deeply in love with her, and now he didn't know what to do with that love.

There was no reason to wake her. No matter how confused he was about everything, the beating she'd taken the night before had been real. The deep-purple bruise on her chin was very real, and it ticked him off that apparently her ex-husband had gotten to her, had beaten her and would have probably killed her if Ben hadn't intervened.

At least she should be safe here. He hated like hell that he had to work the next day, but three deputies were out with the flu, leaving the department too short-handed for him to take the day off. Still, his locks were good and sturdy. He'd tell all of his fellow officers to do frequent drive-bys, but he also wanted them to be working on finding Peter Waverly. That was the only way she would be completely safe.

He turned away from the bedroom and returned to the living room. He sat in his recliner, and Zeus immediately jumped into his lap.

He stroked Zeus's fur. "I know you like her, buddy, but I don't see how this ends." He was so confused and his emotions were still all over the place where she was concerned. If they wound up catching Peter and getting him behind bars, then Colette would be free to pursue her life anywhere with anyone she wanted.

What he feared was that when this was all over, it would once again just be him and Zeus alone again.

PETER SAT ACROSS from Sheila in the busy café. It was dinnertime, and the place was packed. Word had gotten out that Ainsley Meadows had been beaten up the night before by her ex-husband, and all the conversations around him seemed to be about that.

"That's terrible about that poor woman getting beat up," Sheila said as they waited for their orders to be delivered.

"Isn't it though," he said with a straight face.

"Thank God you aren't that kind of man," Sheila said. "All the other men I've been with have beat the hell out of me, but you're nice to me."

Peter forced a smile to his lips. "You're easy to be nice to, Sheila."

"Are you going to score me a little dessert later tonight?" she asked coyly. She looked at him with eyes that begged and burned with need.

He knew "a little dessert" meant drugs. "I'll have to see what's available." Once again he thought of what a pig she was...driven by her addictions and with no desire to change. She disgusted him. She was weak, and he had no understanding or compassion for weak people.

"I'm falling for you, Hank. I've got to say I'm really falling for you." She smiled at him.

Even her smile was a huge turn-off, displaying bad and missing teeth. How could she really believe that a man like him would be remotely interested in a woman like her?

Their food arrived, and they'd only been eating for

a few minutes when two of the deputies from the sheriff's department walked in.

They each had a photo in their hands and they were going from each booth to each table and questioning each and every diner. As one of them, Deputy Nick Marshall, approached his table, Peter felt no tension whatsoever.

He was so much smarter than the law enforcement in this one-pony town. He was smarter than most people. "Evening, folks." Deputy Marshall stepped up next to their table.

"Evening," Peter replied. "What's going on?"

"We're checking with people to see if anyone has seen this man." Deputy Marshall showed Peter a picture of himself. Peter frowned. "No, I haven't seen him."

Sheila looked at the picture and slowly shook her head. "I haven't ever seen him before. Is that the man who beat up the waitress who worked here?"

Deputy Marshall nodded and then looked at Peter once again. "I don't believe we've met."

Peter half rose in his seat and held out his hand. The deputy took his hand and the two men shook. "I'm Hank Bridges. I bought the old pig farm just outside the city limits."

Marshall nodded his head. "I know the place. How long have you been there?"

"Maybe three months or so," he replied. "The place needs a lot of cleanup, and I'm working on it."

"Well, it's nice to meet you and welcome to town," the deputy said and then moved on to the next table.

Peter went back to eating his meal. Oh yes, he was smart enough to know how to get his revenge against the woman who had left him.

He knew where his daughter was, and he knew where Colette was located. He was going to get her. He was going to make her pay. It was just a matter of time. A sweet rush of pleasure shot through him.

"Are you going to eat those French fries?" Sheila asked and gestured to the potatoes left on his plate.

"No, help yourself," he replied and pushed his plate closer to her. *Eat up*, he thought. It would just make the pigs happier. Sheila first…and then Colette.

Oink. Oink.

Chapter Thirteen

Colette awoke to semidarkness in the room. For a moment she was confused as to where she was and what was going on. Then it all slammed back into her.

Peter was someplace in town. She was in Hunter's bed, and Hunter knew all her secrets. She rolled over and sat up and tried to ignore the sharp pain in her wounded ribs. Right now the wound in her heart hurt just as badly.

She got up, and her stomach growled with hunger. She had no idea what time it was, but she hadn't eaten anything all day. While she'd just like to sleep all night to escape her depressing emotions, she was wide-awake now and needed something to eat.

What she really needed was Hunter's arms around her. She needed him to hold her tight against his warm, strong body. She wanted him to whisper in her ear that he loved her and everything was going to be all right. But she knew that wasn't going to happen. He probably hated her now.

She left the bedroom and went into the living room,

where the lights were on in anticipation of nightfall. Hunter wasn't in the living room.

She found him in the kitchen, seated at the table with a cup of coffee before him. As she entered the room, Zeus danced at her feet. She bent down and gave him a quick scratch behind his ears.

"I was wondering how long you might sleep," Hunter said. He got up from the table and walked over to open the back door and let Zeus outside. He then returned to the table.

She stood by the table but didn't sit. "I took a pain pill and only intended to lie down for a few minutes, but I guess I was more tired than I thought."

"You must be starving," he said. She felt his distance in his tone, in the blankness of his eyes. She supposed she should have expected it.

"I am hungry," she replied.

"I thought maybe soup and crackers might sound good to you," he said and got up from the table.

"Actually, that sounds perfect."

"Why don't you sit and I'll get it for you." He pointed to the chair across from where he had been seated.

"You don't have to wait on me," she protested.

"I don't mind. All I need to know is if you want chicken noodle or tomato soup. I'm afraid those are the only kinds I have."

"Tomato sounds good. Thank you." She sat at the table and watched him as he got the can of soup, fixed it in a soup bowl and then put it in the microwave to warm.

As the microwave hummed, Hunter opened a package of crackers and placed a handful of them on a saucer. As he worked, he made no eye contact with her, and a heavy silence hung between them.

A ding announced the soup was ready, and he delivered it to the table in front of her and then added the plate of crackers. "Would you like something to drink?" he asked.

"No, thanks, I'm good. Are you going to sit with me while I eat?"

He sank down in the chair opposite her and looked at a place just over her head. "Did anything happen while I was sleeping?" she asked. She'd hoped somehow a miracle would have happened while she was out and Peter had been caught.

"Nothing, although everyone is looking for Peter," he replied.

He finally looked at her, and in the depths of his eyes she saw not only distrust, but pain...pain that she knew she'd put there.

"Hunter, it was all real for me," she said softly. "I might have lied about my name and where I came from, but I didn't lie about how I feel for you. I'm in love with you, Hunter."

Her words hung in the air for what felt like an eternity. She had hoped she'd see a happy smile curve his lips, a warmth fill his eyes, but neither happened.

He studied her as if she were a scientific specimen he'd never seen before, and then he sighed. "Were you ever going to tell me the truth?" he finally asked.

"Of course I was. I almost told you the night we made love, but then I decided I'd wait until we figured out who was doing the terrible things to me. I was going to tell you, Hunter. I swear I was going to tell you." She realized he had no reason to believe her now.

He sighed once again. "Eat your soup before it gets cold. I'm going to make a phone call to check in with Nick." He got up, let Zeus back into the house, and then he and the dog left the room.

She stared down into her soup, her eyes filling with tears. She should have known this would happen, but someplace in her heart she'd hoped for it to be different. She'd hoped that love conquered all, but she now knew that sometimes love just wasn't enough.

When this was all over, when he remembered her, she would just be another woman who had lied to him. She hated that. She'd managed to do exactly what Juanita had asked her not to do—she'd broken his heart.

Although she no longer felt hungry, she ate the soup and crackers because she knew she needed to put something in her stomach. Tears continued to burn her eyes, but she managed not to cry.

She'd hoped that she and Hunter would share a future together. Now she didn't know what would happen next with her life.

Even if they caught Peter and managed to make charges stick, she didn't think she could stay in Dusty Gulch if she and Hunter weren't together. It would just be too painful to see him every day, to love him every day and know that he no longer felt the same way about her.

When she finished eating, she carried the bowl and saucer to the sink, rinsed them off and then loaded them into the dishwasher.

She left the kitchen and found Hunter seated in his recliner with Zeus next to him. She sat on the sofa and looked at him. "Did you check in with Nick?"

"I did, but so far there is nothing new to report."

"I suppose you hate me right now," she said.

"Ainsley...Colette...I could never hate you." A whisper of warmth filled his eyes. It was there for only a moment and then was gone. A frown cut across his forehead. "Right now the only thing I'm focused on is getting your ex-husband behind bars."

"And once that happens?"

"I don't know." He looked down at Zeus and stroked his fur, then returned his gaze to her. "To be perfectly honest, I'm kind of numb right now where you're concerned. I haven't really had time to process everything you've told me today."

"Do you think time will help you to forgive me?" Her heart raced in her chest as she waited for his answer. Was there any hope at all that they would be together when this was all over?

"I don't know how to answer that right now. All I want at the moment is for you to be safe." He held her gaze for a long moment and then looked back down at Zeus. "I need time, Ains...Colette. I just need time."

"I understand," she replied. And she did. She knew

all the lies she'd told him had come out of left field. She hated that it had all unfolded the way it had.

She drew in a deep breath and winced as her ribs protested. "Would it be easier if I moved back to my apartment or someplace else?" she asked.

"No," he replied sharply. "You need to be here." His gaze softened. "This is the best place for you right now. Even though I have to work in the morning, I've already instructed drive-bys by my fellow officers at regular intervals to make sure nothing happens here. Besides, your ex would be foolish to try something now. He's got to know by now that he's on the hot seat. I wouldn't be surprised if he's already hours away from here."

"I hope he isn't hours away. I hope this time he's overplayed his hand and believed in his own invulnerability and has stuck around. If he goes into the wind, then I'll never find peace. He tried to kill me last night, and he'll never stop trying until he's succeeded."

"I thought he'd killed you last night." Pain leaped into his eyes. "Some of the longest hours of my life were waiting to hear from the doctor after you'd been taken to the hospital."

She was so damned selfish, she realized. She'd been caught up in her own drama and hadn't realized what Hunter had been through in the last twenty-four hours.

She now saw the lines of exhaustion on his face. How late had he been up the night before…waiting to hear from the doctor…and then worrying about her recovery?

"Did you manage to get any rest while I was sleeping?" she asked.

"No, I'm not much of a daytime napper. I'll sleep tonight," he replied.

"Are you sure you don't want to sleep in the bedroom and let me have the sofa?" she asked.

"I'll be fine on the sofa," he replied firmly. "So, you mentioned that your mother is alive and you have a sister. Was that the imaginary sister you spoke about?"

"Everything I said about her was true except the part about her being imaginary." She sighed, and tears once again began to burn in her eyes as she thought of her mother and her sister.

"We've always been very close. When I first went on the run from Peter, I was communicating with them regularly, but then Peter appeared in the small town we were staying in and I realized he had to have been tapping their phones. We managed to leave town before he found where we were staying, and after that I realized I had to never contact my mom and sister again."

She swallowed hard against her tears. "I needed to do whatever I could to keep Melinda away from Peter. If he gets his hands on her, he'll eventually destroy her."

"I'm sorry you've had to make the choices that you have," he said. His eyes filled with compassion. "That's no way for a woman, for a child to live."

"I thought I was finally safe here," she said with a touch of bitterness. "Melinda loves it here, and we were hoping to make it our forever home."

"If we catch Peter, you could still make this your forever home," he said. Once again he looked down at the dog, making it impossible for her to read any emotion that might emanate from his beautiful eyes.

She released another sigh. "We'll see."

She couldn't see into the future, and Hunter wasn't giving any clue as to whether there was any hope for them to come out of this as a couple. Right now it felt unlikely that they would come out of it together. That thought made her want to leave, to run from all the memories of him and love that were in this small town.

But she had Melinda to think about. Melinda loved it here. She'd made good friends and loved school, and it was difficult to contemplate tearing her away from all those good things just because Colette couldn't suck it up and figure out how to live here without Hunter in her life.

She could only hope that with time, Hunter would forgive her and love her once again.

Hunter breathed a deep sigh of relief once Colette finally left the living room to unpack and go to bed. Their conversations had been difficult, and he knew she wanted something from him that he just couldn't give her right now.

Everything he'd learned about her was just too new. She'd lied to him about so many things—how was he to trust that what she was saying to him now was true?

This wasn't over with yet, and it was in her best interest to keep him emotionally close to her. If they got

Peter behind bars, then would she confess that she'd lied about loving Hunter? Would she then admit that she'd only been using him?

God, he was so confused. But one thing he wasn't confused about—he wanted Peter Waverly behind bars and facing attempted murder charges for what he'd done to her last night.

He grabbed a blanket and a spare bed pillow from his hallway closet. He tossed them on the sofa and then turned out all the lights except for the light above the stove. If she got up in the middle of the night for a drink of water, at least she'd be able to see what she was doing.

With his gun on the coffee table, he finally got out of his clothes except for his boxers and then stretched out on the sofa with Zeus at his feet.

He was utterly exhausted and yet sleep remained elusive. He found himself thinking about his marriage to Emily. She'd been his high school sweetheart and as far as he was concerned one of the prettiest girls in town.

He'd thought he knew her inside and out. The one thing he hadn't known was just how duplicitous she was. Lies had fallen so easily from her lips, lies that he'd believed because he wanted to so badly.

When she'd left their marriage, he'd walled up his heart, built sturdy fences inside him so that nobody could ever hurt him like that again.

And then he'd met Ainsley Meadows, a woman he'd believed was open and honest, a woman he believed would be his future. And she'd shattered his trust all over again.

He understood the reasons she'd chosen to live undercover, and he recognized why she'd lied to him. But emotionally he was having trouble wrapping his head around things.

Right now he was afraid to tap back into the love he'd had for her. He was afraid to feel at all. All he wanted to focus on for the moment was finding Peter. He wanted to make sure that from this point on Colette and Melinda would be safe from the man who was obviously a brutal monster.

He finally fell asleep and into nightmares of Peter chasing Colette down a dark street. Peter wielded a long knife that glittered in a streetlamp. Hunter held his gun in his hand. He fired it at Peter, only to discover his gun held no bullets.

Knowing he needed to get to Peter before the man could kill Colette, Hunter tried to run, but his feet and legs refused to move. He jerked awake covered in a cold sweat and panting as if he'd just run a marathon.

He swung his feet over the edge of the sofa, aware that the first stir of morning was peeking over the horizon. Zeus sat up and yawned and then jumped down from the sofa.

Hunter got up and let him out the back door and then started a pot of coffee. He was up about an hour earlier than he usually got up on workdays, but there was no way he wanted to doze off again and fall back into the nightmares that had chased him all night long.

Once he got the coffee working, he then went into the office where he'd hung several of his uniforms before Colette had taken over his room. He grabbed one of them and then headed for the shower.

After washing off he remained standing beneath a hot spray of water as if it had the power to unjumble his thoughts. Unfortunately it didn't help.

Once he was finished showering and then dressing, he returned to the kitchen. He let Zeus back inside, poured himself a cup of coffee and sank down at the kitchen table.

He hated having to go in to work today, but one more deputy on the streets made the odds of them finding Peter that much better. However, he believed the man had probably left town. He'd be stupid to stay knowing that everyone in the area was looking for him.

If he had left town and wasn't captured in the next day or two, then Colette would remain at risk. He frowned and sipped his coffee, the idea unsettling to him. How could she live with the threat of him killing her continuing to hang over her head?

How had she lived for the past three years? The mental, the emotional pressure on her had to have been so intense. Had she gone to bed every night with terror on her mind? Had that terror ever released its grip on her?

Compassion for her situation, for what she'd been through and what she might still have to endure, fluttered through him. God, he wished it could end for her here, but there was no guarantee it would.

And then what?

That's the part he couldn't think about right now.

He'd just poured his second cup of coffee when Colette came into the kitchen. She was already dressed in a pair of pink jogging pants and a matching sweatshirt. Her long dark hair was damp, letting him know she'd already showered in the master bath.

The bruise on her lower jaw appeared even more livid this morning. The sight of it made him want to slam his fist into Peter Waverly's face.

"Hmm, that coffee smells wonderful," she said.

"Have a seat and I'll pour you a cup."

"Nonsense, just tell me where the cups are and I can get it."

"Right cabinet above the sink," he replied.

As she walked by him, he caught a whiff of her scent…a clean smell coupled with the hint of her perfume. His stomach tightened with tension in response. Even knowing all the lies she'd told him, his body still yearned for hers. It was his mind that was having problems sorting his emotions out.

She got her coffee and then joined him at the table. "Did you sleep well?" she asked.

"I slept okay." He wasn't about to share with her the nightmares he'd suffered. "What about you?"

"I slept all right."

"You're up early."

"I'm used to being up early to open the café. What time do you go in to work this morning?" She took a sip of the coffee. Above the cup her beguiling eyes begged him to let her back into his thoughts…his heart.

He steeled himself against them. He wasn't ready to untangle his emotions where she was concerned. "I need to leave here around seven thirty or so."

"There's enough time for me to make you some breakfast," she said. "I mean, if I'm not overstepping kitchen privileges."

He couldn't help but smile. "For as long as you're here, you have full kitchen privileges. And while I appreciate the offer, I'm not much of a breakfast eater. Feel free to help yourself to whatever you want."

"I'm not much of a breakfast eater, either. Coffee is good enough for me." She raised the cup for another drink.

"Do you know how to shoot a gun?"

Her eyes widened in surprise, and she lowered the cup to the table. "Point and pull the trigger. That's all I know about guns. Why?"

"I've got a nine millimeter that's for my personal use. I'm going to leave it here for you. Could you actually shoot your ex-husband?"

Her eyes narrowed. "Absolutely. I know his only goal is to kill me, so I could absolutely shoot him to save myself."

He believed her. Her eyes burned with determination. "I'll be right back." He got up from the table and went into the room he used as an office.

He grabbed his keys and unlocked the right top drawer. Inside was the spare gun he kept for security purposes. He took the gun out of the drawer, checked it to make sure the safety was on, and then he carried it back into the kitchen.

As he set it on the table with the barrel facing the wall, she looked at it soberly and then looked up at him. "I can't believe it's come to this," she said softly.

"To be perfectly honest, my gut instinct is he's left town. I think they would have caught him by now if he was still in Dusty Gulch. However, just in case I'm wrong, I want you to be able to protect yourself while you're here alone. Before I leave to go to work, I'll take the safety off so all you have to do is point and pull the trigger."

She nodded. "Aim for center mass, right?"

"Right," he replied, surprised she knew the term.

She grinned at him. "I picked that up while watching police shows on television."

Her grin caught him off guard, and a well of love for her rose up inside him. He stared down into his coffee cup. Damn her for ruining things. Damn her for not telling him the truth as soon as they started seriously dating each other. Damn her for twisting and tangling his emotions to the point where he didn't know what to feel.

"Center mass is right," he now replied. For a moment they sipped their coffee in silence. Then she looked at him, and all her features softened. A soft pleading filled her eyes.

"Hunter…" she began.

He held up his hand. "Don't."

"Don't what?"

It would be so easy to fall into the blue depths of her winsome eyes, but he couldn't allow himself. "Colette, I don't want any heart-to-heart discussions right now. I can't think about us right now."

He saw the pain that dimmed the brightness in her eyes, and he hated himself for putting it there. But at the moment, he didn't know if they had a path forward or not. The last thing he wanted to do was give her any false hope about what might happen between them in the future.

"I just want to tell you thank-you for letting me stay here and for keeping me safe," she finally replied.

"Protect and serve, that's our motto."

"We both know you're going way above your duty," she replied. "You're a great deputy, and you're a wonderful, good man."

He didn't feel like a good man right now. He still felt numb. Once again they fell into an uncomfortable silence. She looked at the clock over the stove and got up from the table. "I'm just going to go back and call Juanita's to check in on Melinda before school."

He drew a deep breath as she left the kitchen. There was no question that things were going to be awkward between them. Sharing space with so many things unresolved between them was going to create more than a little bit of tension.

When it was time for him to leave for work, he was torn with the desire to get out on the streets and find Peter and remain here with her to make sure she stayed safe.

"Make sure you only touch the trigger if you intend to shoot somebody," he said as he took the safety of the gun off. "Where do you want to keep it?"

"How about on the coffee table. I plan on spending most of the day in the living room."

He placed the gun on the coffee table. "You know how to use the television. Help yourself to anything you want to eat, and I'll bring home dinner for us from the café."

"I would be glad to cook something for us," she offered.

"I'd rather just bring something home. Is there anything in particular you'd like?" As silly as it sounded, he didn't want her to cook dinner for them. It felt too intimate...too much like they were a cozy couple.

"Anything is fine. Just surprise me." She walked with him to the front door. He started to go out the door, but she stopped him by placing her hand on his arm. "Hunter, stay safe today."

"Always," he replied with a reassuring smile. "If you get scared or something doesn't seem right, call me. One of the other deputies or I will come running."

"I'm sure I'll be fine," she replied.

He wanted to touch her. He wanted to pull her into his arms and hold her tight. He needed to run a finger down the side of her soft cheek or touch a strand of her silky hair. He didn't do any of those things.

"Lock the door behind me, and I'll see you later

today." He practically ran out of the house with the need to escape her. It was crazy, but he'd rather face down a psycho killer than face his emotions where Colette was concerned.

Chapter Fourteen

The minute Hunter left, he seemed to take all the oxygen, all the life out of the air with him. She locked the front door and then went into the living room and sat on the edge of the sofa.

She stared at the gun on the coffee table. Could she shoot to kill her ex-husband, the father of her child? As she thought of all the times he'd beaten her, of the intense mental and physical pain he'd put her through, the answer was easy. Yes, she could definitely shoot to kill him.

More important than the crimes Peter had already perpetrated against her were the crimes she feared he would perpetrate against their daughter. For that alone Colette could kill him.

If Peter really had left town, then a new nearly insurmountable issue would arise. How could she continue to stay here if he knew where she was? Even if Hunter forgave her and professed his love for her, how could she stay if Peter got away?

She turned on the television in an attempt to escape

her depressing thoughts. Hopefully, in the next couple of days, she would know whether Peter was truly gone from the area. Then she would have to make a decision about what to do next.

She had told Hunter she'd slept well, but that wasn't exactly the truth. She'd had trouble getting comfortable. Her ribs hurt and the bruise on her chin throbbed with pain, keeping her awake off and on throughout the night. And if the physical pain hadn't been enough, she'd been unable to turn off her thoughts.

She found a channel with a game show on. She kept the volume fairly low so she could hear any other noises throughout the house. Zeus jumped up on the sofa next to her and curled up at her side.

She stroked his soft fur and tried to keep her mind empty, but it was impossible. She'd dreamed of living here with Hunter and Zeus and Melinda. She'd dreamed of them all being a happy family.

She definitely owed her daughter a big apology for not believing her about her father speaking to her at night. Who could have guessed it was true, that Peter had installed all the equipment in the café attic?

Shoving away these thoughts, she tried to focus on the game show. At noon she let Zeus out of the back door and then opened the refrigerator to find something for lunch.

She'd hoped to hear from Hunter by now and learn that Peter had been found and arrested, but apparently there was nothing new to report. She found a can of tuna in the pantry and made herself a sandwich with chips for lunch.

When she was finished eating, she walked to the front windows and peered outside. She knew from talking with Hunter that most of his neighbors worked and weren't home during the days.

She saw nothing amiss in the area. As she stood there, a patrol car slowly drove by and then disappeared down the street. With a sigh she turned away and walked to the back door to let Zeus back inside.

The dog danced in, followed by a man she'd seen often in the café. "Hank, what are you doing here? What do you want?" Why would Hank Bridges be here? Why had he just come through Hunter's back door?

"Hello, Colette."

The familiar voice shot disbelief through her. She stared at him. Her brain froze. No wonder they hadn't been able to find him. He looked nothing like the photo she'd given to them. He was the new man in town… he'd walked the sidewalks free and easy, he'd eaten several times in the café with Sheila Turrel. Peter!

She stumbled backward from the door. The sight of him here and now shot sheer terror through her.

The gun. She had to get to the gun. She turned to run, but he caught her leg and she fell to the floor. She rolled over on her back and kicked at him. Zeus barked as if to protest what was going on.

He backed up a bit from her and laughed. "Ah, Colette, I've so looked forward to this reunion."

"Go away, Peter," she said breathlessly. "Just leave me alone."

He laughed again, the sound shooting arctic chills up her spine. "Now you know that isn't going to happen. You have to pay for leaving me, for taking my daughter away from me."

"You don't care about Melinda. You never loved her or me."

"Love has nothing to do with this. You belonged to me." He leaned over her and grinned.

She had to get to the gun. She'd been stupid to open the door without the weapon in her hand. She needed to get up. She kicked at him again, needing to gain some distance to get to her feet and run for the gun.

He kicked her, connecting with the rib he'd broken. Pain screamed through her, blurring her vision as she lost her breath.

Before she could fully recover, he grabbed her by her hair and yanked her up to her feet. She screamed but knew there was nobody who would hear her. She was vaguely aware of Zeus running from the room.

"You want that gun?" he whispered in her ear. His grip on her hair tightened. "You want to get that gun and shoot me?" He punched her in her side. Once again pain ripped through her, weakening her knees. "That wouldn't be nice, Colette."

His hot, stale breath made her want to throw up. "If anyone is going to shoot somebody, it's going to be me shooting you. But that would be too easy."

He pulled out a syringe. New horror swept through

her. She fought to get away, but he stabbed the needle into her arm.

She flailed her arms and kicked at him, desperate to get free. He laughed at her efforts, his laughter sounding like the devil's happiness.

Within minutes her arms began to feel too heavy to fight and her legs could barely hold her up. What had he given to her? Oh God, what had been in the syringe?

Her eyelids grew heavy. He loosened his grip on her hair, and she nearly fell against him. *Help*, her mind screamed. He laughed as he picked her up in his arms.

He'd won. That was the last thought that drifted through her mind before she knew no more.

HER HEAD POUNDED. Her mouth was dry. Colette came to in confusion. She opened her eyes and frowned. She was in a kitchen she'd never seen before. The floor was an old, faded linoleum, and an old table stood in front of a window with a cracked pane of glass. The air held an unpleasant odor.

Where was she? She tried to raise a hand to her head and realized she was tied to the chair. That's when everything crashed back into her head. Peter…who didn't look like Peter…the stab of the needle in her arm… Oh God, she was in trouble. Peter was actually Hank Bridges, and nobody knew that.

As if to punctuate that thought, Peter walked into the kitchen. He grabbed a chair, flipped it around backward and sat directly in front of her. "Hello, Colette."

It was so disconcerting to hear the familiar voice

coming out of the unfamiliar face. But the eyes were the same, dark blue eyes that burned with evil intent.

"Aren't you going to tell me how happy you are to see me again?"

She kept her mouth shut. She had no desire to engage with him in any way. If he was waiting for her to beg and plead for her life, it wasn't going to happen.

How long had she been unconscious? Did Hunter know yet that she was missing from the house? Were they all out looking for her now?

They'd never find her. They could look everywhere, but they'd never suspect she was here. They were all looking for Peter, not this new, improved version of her ex-husband.

She wanted to weep with defeat, but she didn't want to give him the satisfaction of seeing her tears. He'd always gotten off on seeing her cry.

"Gee, I guess you aren't talking to me. Maybe I can make you scream." He started to stand up from the chair.

"Of course you can make me scream. You've got me tied to a chair and helpless. Congratulations, big man. You're a real hero."

The slap snapped her head to the side. She bit her bottom lip to keep from crying out. "Show me some respect. I've gone to a lot of trouble to get you here," he said. "I've spent hundreds of thousands of dollars to make this happen."

"Why, Peter? After all this time, why come after me at all?" she asked. Her hands were tied behind her back, and she twisted and turned them in an effort to gain some give in the rope.

"You belong to me. Don't you remember that was our song? We danced to it at our wedding."

"We divorced," she replied. "And I never belonged to you. I belong to myself."

She hadn't intended to talk to him, but she now realized she needed to keep him talking. She needed time, time for somebody to find her. She desperately hoped somebody—anybody—would find her.

"A piece of paper doesn't change the fact that you belong to me," he said.

She sighed in frustration. "Why did you marry me in the first place?" she asked.

"I married you because I wanted you. I knew after our first date that you were the woman I wanted to bear my children, the woman I wanted to spend my life with. Why did you marry me?" He looked at her in amusement.

"I fell in love with you, Peter. I thought you were a good man, a gentle man who would take care of me and any children we had. But you became a cruel and abusive man." She stiffened, waiting for another blow from him.

"That's because you failed to live up to my expectations of you as a wife." His eyes were dark and flat, like the eyes of a serpent. "You had to be taught, Colette. It wasn't my fault that you were a slow learner. I hope our daughter doesn't need to be taught."

She wanted to tear his eyes out, stab him in his sick,

black heart. As she thought of Melinda in his care, she wanted to scream at the injustice of evil winning. Peter would steal all the sweetness, all the happiness out of Melinda.

Colette would gladly spend a thousand years in hell to save Melinda from him. But the devil was already working with Peter. "Please just let me go, Peter. I'll make sure you get plenty of visitation with Melinda."

"Why should I settle for visitation when I can have her full-time?"

"Please, Peter. If you ever loved me, then just let me go." She had thought she wasn't going to beg, but she was now begging for her life…for Melinda's life. "I won't tell anyone what you look like or that you're living as Hank Bridges. Your identity is safe with me."

His eyes burned into hers. "You were my everything, Colette. I needed you as much as I needed air to breathe."

"You tried to kill me," she replied half hysterically. She continued to work at loosening the rope holding her hands, but so far she'd had no success. Her fingers were numb, but her wrists felt raw and painful. "Peter, you stabbed me in my stomach. You almost killed me."

"I'll admit my need to discipline you got a little out of hand, but that didn't give you the right to leave me. You were mine, and you'll be mine until you die."

He stood abruptly and shoved the chair he'd been sitting in aside. "The only way I'll truly be free of you is for you to be gone…dead. That's the price you pay for leaving me, Colette."

He stalked over to the nearby door and yanked it open. Immediately a noxious smell wafted in the air. Squeals and grunts could be heard.

Peter turned to look at her. "Hear that? Those are my pets. Did you know that sixteen pigs can completely eat a human being in eight minutes? There are twenty-five starving pigs in my pen. I tested the information with Ted, who got me access to the café attic." She stared at him in horror.

"It actually took seven and a half minutes for Ted to get crunched up and swallowed. Then this morning they got fed again. Poor old Sheila was another loose end that needed to be taken care of. I figure by late this evening the pigs will be hungry again." He grinned at her. "Of course I'll feed my pets...I'm going to feed them you."

As he turned and left the kitchen, she worked desperately on trying to free her hands. She was horrified not only by what he'd already done but also what he planned to do to her.

THEY HAD SCOURED the town for Peter Waverly and nobody professed to have seen him. "How can one man stay so far under the radar?" Hunter asked Nick when they were both in the office for a few minutes.

"You got me." Nick shook his head. "We checked the motel and the few places in town that are rented out. We've asked people if they've noticed anyone in or around their barns and outbuildings, and we've come up empty-handed. We're going to start checking on some of the abandoned buildings in the area, but if you want my opinion, I think he's probably left town."

"That's the last thing Ains...Colette wanted." Hunter frowned.

"This all must have been a shock to you. How are you doing with it all?" Nick asked.

Hunter drew in a deep breath. "To be honest, I don't know how I'm doing with it all. Right now I want to stay focused on minimizing any danger toward her."

"And after that?" Nick asked.

"After that I don't know," Hunter replied honestly. "I kind of feel the same way I did when I realized all the lies Emily had told me."

"But there's a difference. Emily lied to deceive you so she could continue her affair. Colette lied to save her and her daughter's lives."

Nick's words haunted Hunter during the rest of the morning as he worked street patrol. Yes, there was a difference. He tried to put himself in Colette's position. What lengths would he go to in order to protect Danny if the little boy had lived?

He would have lied, stolen and done whatever necessary to save his son from danger. Why would he hold it against Colette for doing the same thing?

It was just after noon when his phone rang and he saw George's caller ID. Why on earth would George be calling him right now?

"Hey, George, what's going on?"

"Hunter, I got something to tell you...something really, really important."

"What's that?" Hunter asked. George had spoken superfast, and Hunter wondered if perhaps George was off his meds again. He didn't sound drunk—rather he sounded amped up.

"I thought today was your day off and I spent most of the morning thinning out some plants and I repotted some because I thought you might like them." The words spewed out of George so fast Hunter could barely digest them. The man was obviously agitated about something.

"So, I took them down to your house and was just about to knock on the door when I heard two people talking inside and then I heard the side gate in your backyard open. I...I peeked around the corner of the house and saw him—he was...he was carrying Ainsley over his shoulder."

A sick burst of adrenaline shot through Hunter. "Who was it, George? Who was carrying her outside?" he asked urgently.

"I can't remember. I know him from somewhere... but right now I can't remember from where. Dammit, I knew she was in trouble and I hid behind the bushes like a damned coward. I'm sorry, Hunter. I'm so sorry. You needed me to save her and I...I failed you." He began to weep.

"George, where are you now?" Hunter asked as he turned his car around to head for home.

"I'm at your house on the front porch."

"I'll be right there." Hunter hung up and raced for home. How in the hell had a man they were all looking for managed to get to Colette? How had this happened? Oh God, where had Peter taken her?

As he drove, he called Nick to let him know what had happened, and the lawman agreed to meet Hunter at his house. Hunter stepped on the gas, his heart thundering so hard he could hear the frantic beats in his head. Dammit, he'd thought she'd be safe in his house. He shouldn't have worked today no matter how much he was needed to do patrol. He should have stayed with her, kept her near to him.

The good news was there was an eyewitness to the kidnapping. The bad news was the witness could be off his medications and might never be able to identify whom he had seen.

Chapter Fifteen

Hunter drove faster than he'd ever driven through town in his life. He was painfully aware that seconds mattered...minutes mattered. The faster George could tell them something, anything about the kidnapper, the faster they might be able to find Colette.

Peter had already beaten her up. Hunter knew the man wouldn't blink twice before killing her. He could have killed her right there in the house, and yet he'd carried her out and away. Why not just kill her?

Where could he have taken her? Where was his lair? The man had apparently moved freely through town in order to leave the items on Colette's porch and to leave the note in the café. Why had everyone who was questioned in town indicated they had never seen Peter anywhere before? Why hadn't he seen Peter in town? The man was obviously a freaking ghost.

Hunter screeched around the corner of the street that led to his house. When he got close enough, he saw George sitting on the front porch. He whirled into his driveway, cut the engine and leaped out of the car.

George stood, tears trekking down his cheeks. "I'm sorry, Hunter. I'm so sorry I didn't do anything to help. I should have tackled him. I should have done something, but I hid like a baby."

"It's okay, George. Right now what I need for you to do is calm down," Hunter said even though he was anything but calm. Every nerve in his body was screaming that he needed to find Colette as soon as possible.

"Come on inside. I need to get some information from you." Hunter tried to stay calm, knowing that would also calm George down, but Hunter wanted to scream with urgency at the only man who had seen Peter Waverly.

As they walked through the living room, Hunter saw the gun still on the coffee table. Obviously she'd never gotten a chance to use it to protect herself. Zeus danced at his feet, and he let the dog out the back door as Nick entered the house.

George began to weep again as Hunter guided him to a seat at the table. "George, we need you to calm down so you can think clearly," Hunter said and tried to keep the panic out of his voice. "You need to tell us exactly what you saw."

"I saw him carrying her over his shoulder," George said.

"Did he have a vehicle waiting for him?" Nick asked.

George nodded. "A black pickup truck. He put her in the passenger seat and then he sped away." Hunter's stomach tightened. Sped away where? Where was the bastard hiding out?

"Was it this man who took her?" Nick showed George the picture of Peter.

"No, it wasn't him," George replied with a frown.

Hunter looked at Nick in confusion. If it wasn't Peter Waverly, then who had taken her away? Were they dealing with two different people? Two separate perpetrators?

George raised a fist and hit himself in the forehead. "I know the man who took her…I just…right now I can't remember who he is. I know I met him. Damn, damn, damn!" He hit himself in the head once again.

Hunter caught his hand. "George, stop hitting yourself. That's not going to get us anywhere. Just give yourself a minute to breathe, a minute to think."

Seconds…minutes…where was she? Hunter's need to find her burned in his belly as his heart continued to beat the rapid rhythm of despair. He needed George to remember, otherwise they had nothing.

"What did the man look like?" he asked.

"Dark hair…nice-looking man." George's frown deepened, and then he snapped his fingers and sat up straighter in his chair. "I know now. I met him at the café. Hank…Hank Bridges. He bought that old pig farm south of town."

Before George was completely finished speaking, Nick and Hunter jumped up from the table and ran outside to their patrol cars.

The pig farm. She'd told them the person who had

beaten her had a strange, unpleasant odor about them. A man living on a pig farm would have had that smell clinging to him.

Hank Bridges. What in the hell did he have to do with Peter Waverly? Was he a hired killer working for Peter? Had Peter been living with Hank? Was that how he had stayed under their radar?

It was much easier for Hunter to focus on these kinds of questions than the questions that ate at his guts. Questions like, were they already too late? Had Peter been waiting at the pig farm to bring him Colette and had he already killed his ex-wife? Was Colette already dead?

Oh God, he could scarcely stand the thought that she might no longer be in this world. He couldn't imagine never again seeing her beautiful smile or hearing her sweet laughter. He couldn't imagine her not being there for her daughter.

His heart hurt. All he wanted was for her to be in his arms. He wanted to bury his face in her sweet-smelling hair, feel her heart beating steady against his own. More than anything he wanted her to be alive.

He got on the radio with Nick. "We need to go in quiet," he said. "We don't know whether there's one or two men in there, but either one of them is capable of killing her."

"I've already called in a couple more men and told them to meet us at the old Winchell place next to the pig farm," Nick said.

Thankfully he didn't mention the fact that they

might already be too late, that they'd reach the farm and find her dead body and the men would already be gone, never to be seen again.

He gripped the steering wheel tightly. Wasn't it enough that he'd had to say goodbye to Danny? Hadn't life taken enough from him already? He'd lost both his wife and his baby boy. Dammit, he didn't want to lose Colette as well.

Nick followed him down the highway that would take them to the Winchell place, a small farm where the Winchell family had lived and struggled for years. Three years ago they had given up, moved away and abandoned the place to the bank. Nobody had lived in the place since.

He turned in to the long driveway and drove up far enough that the vehicles wouldn't be seen from the road. Nick pulled in behind him, and within minutes two more patrol cars joined them. Deputies Greg McCain and Barry Simpson got out of the cars.

"What's the plan?" Hunter asked Nick, recognizing that ultimately Nick was the lead on the case.

"We need to get close enough to do a little recon," Nick said. "We need to figure out who, exactly, is in the house and where they are in the place. Greg, why don't you and I sneak closer and see what we can see? Hunter, you and Barry wait here. We'll check back here and we can make our ultimate plan to move in."

Before Hunter could protest, the two men were gone, cutting through an overgrown cornfield in the direction of the pig farm. "There isn't time for this,"

her want to melt into them. His face displayed so much of the character of the man he was. His warm eyes and laugh lines showed him for the good man he was.

Whether he ever found love for her again, she hoped with the information he had about Peter, he would somehow keep Peter from gaining custody of her daughter. She would also hope that after her death he would find forgiveness for the lies she'd told him in an effort to survive.

She wanted to weep for all the dreams she'd wanted to build with Hunter, dreams of happiness and family that had all been shattered. Still, she would take her last breath loving him. She would love him through eternity.

She opened her eyes and tensed as Peter came into the room once again. "It's time, Colette. It's time you pay the ultimate price for running from me. My pigs are very hungry, and I'm eager to end this and get on with my life with my darling daughter."

She fought back a shiver. "You'll burn in hell for everything you have done," she said fervently.

He laughed. "Maybe, but in the meantime I'm having such a wonderful time." He moved behind her and began to untie her hands. "Oof, I see you've been a bad girl and tried to get loose. You've got your hands all bloody, but that's okay. My pet pigs absolutely love blood."

Once he had her untied, he grabbed her by the arm and yanked her upright. She immediately fell to the floor on her butt. There was no way she was going to make this easy for him.

"Get up," he commanded, anger rife in his voice.

She no longer feared his anger. What was he going to do to her? She was going to die within minutes anyway. "Make me," she replied.

He yanked harder on her arm, but she made herself deadweight. "Don't be childish, Colette. Now stand up before I lose my patience."

"What are you going to do if I don't? Kill me?" She laughed. She had nothing to lose now. "You're pathetic, Peter. You're a loser who has wasted the last three years of your life chasing after a woman who didn't give you a second thought. You might have wanted me, but I never, ever wanted you."

Peter's face reddened, letting her know she was making him very, very angry. "Shut up," he yelled.

"Why should I shut up? You've been talking to me the whole time you've had me here. Now it's my turn to talk. You were a terrible husband, Peter. You're a little man who is abusive to women. You really think you're a big man because you can slap around a woman? Because you can get a knife and stab me? You abused me throughout our whole marriage. I ran from you because I hated you and I never, ever wanted to see you again. Even if you hadn't tried to stab me to death, I would have left you anyway. You don't deserve the love of any good woman, and you definitely don't deserve my beautiful daughter."

"Are you through?" A muscle ticked in his jaw.

"Not quite." She drew in a deep breath and laughed. "You also sucked in bed."

She barely got the words out of her mouth when he slammed his fist into the side of her face. An intense pain caused bright lights to flash in her brain, and then there was nothing.

"THERE'S ONLY TWO of them in the house," Nick said breathlessly. He and Greg had just come back to where Hunter and Barry had waited. "It's just Colette and Hank Bridges. We saw no sign of Peter Waverly."

"Was she alive?" Tension pressed tight in Hunter's chest.

Nick nodded affirmatively, and a rush of relief swept through Hunter. "She's tied to a chair in the kitchen," Nick said.

"If there's just one person with her, then this should be an easy takedown," Barry said.

"Are you sure there was nobody else in the house?" Hunter asked.

"Positive. We got eyes on all the rooms in the house. There's nobody else there." Nick looked at Barry. "And there's nothing easy about this. Hank is obviously a dangerous man. If he hears or sees us coming, there's nothing to stop him from killing Colette."

Hunter didn't know what the deal was with Hank Bridges. He and Peter Waverly had to somehow be in cahoots. Hank could only be looked at as an assassin who had been paid to kill Colette. All Hunter really knew was one false move and Colette would die.

"We need to go in carefully and use the element of surprise to take down Hank," Nick said. "Barry, do you have the door ram in your trunk?"

"I do."

"Okay, I'll take it and go in the front door. Greg, you take the south side of the house, and Barry, you take the north side. Hunter, you go around to the back. That's where the kitchen is located. We not only want to get Colette out of there, but I also want to get Hank under arrest," Nick said. "Earbuds in and I'll give the signal to move in when I think everyone is in place."

The four of them took off, moving as silently as they could through the field. Hunter's heart raced with the need to get her out of the farmhouse and to safety. He hoped and prayed that this rescue effort didn't go wrong. One mistake and he knew Colette would die.

Every muscle, every single nerve in his body tensed as a rush of adrenaline flooded through his veins. His need to get to her before anything happened was single-focused and overwhelming.

He changed his direction to come around to the back of the old farmhouse. There was no way to predict what Hank would do when he realized the police were on top of him.

And where was Peter Waverly? Where was the man behind all this? There was no doubt in Hunter's mind that Colette's ex-husband had orchestrated everything that had happened to her. So, where was he? He would think a man with such focus on killing a woman would want to be present when she died.

Still, he couldn't think about that right now. All he wanted to do was bust down the doors, release Colette and hold her warm, breathing body against his.

As he got closer, the smell of the pigs grew stronger. Hunter had been around pigs before, and normally they didn't smell so unpleasant. But this was the odor of neglected animals, of filth and waste.

When this was all over, Hunter would make sure the pigs were removed by the humane society so they could be placed with farmers who would properly care for them.

The farmhouse came into his view. A shed sat between the edge of the backyard and the house, a perfect place for Hunter to take cover until he got the signal to move in.

Keeping low and moving fast, Hunter raced for the small building. He slammed his back against it and held his breath, waiting to see if anyone in the house had possibly seen him.

When the air remained quiet, he breathed a sigh of relief. So far…so good. The only sound was the grunting and rustling coming from the pigpen.

He froze as he heard the sound of the back door opening. He peeked around the corner of the shed and saw Hank with a prone Colette across his shoulder.

What the hell? Was she already dead? Horror screamed through Hunter as he suddenly realized the man's intent. The pigs squealed as Hank raised Colette high enough to throw her over the porch railing and into the pen.

"Move in. Move in," Hunter screamed through his radio as he raced toward the pen.

Hank looked up in stunned surprise. "Put her down, Hank. Put her down on the porch," Hunter yelled as he drew his weapon.

Hank froze. Colette looked like a limp rag doll in his big arms. "Put her down on the porch!" Hunter yelled again and ran across the lawn toward the two.

"She belongs with the pigs," Hank yelled back. Once again he raised her up to his shoulders. "Say goodbye to Colette," he said and laughed.

A crack sounded in the air, and Hank's laughter stopped abruptly. As if in slow motion, he sank down to his knees and spilled Colette out of his arms and onto the porch.

Nick stepped out of the house and onto the porch, his gun in his hand and a bullet hole through the screen door. Hunter stumbled forward, his sole concern the woman lying lifeless on the deck. Was she already dead? Had they been too late after all?

His heart nearly stopped as he finally crouched down beside her and felt for a pulse. *Let there be one... please let there be one*, his mind begged.

Her face looked red and bruised, and if Hank Bridges wasn't next to him dead, then Hunter would have killed him with his bare hands.

"She's got a pulse," he cried out to Nick. "We need an ambulance out here."

"Already been called in," Nick replied.

Hunter moved around so he was cradling her head

in his lap. "What did he do to her?" he breathed more to himself than to anyone else. Had she been drugged? "The bastard was going to throw her in with the pigs."

"That's why I shot him," Nick replied. "I was afraid he was about to toss her right in, and those pigs look like they are starving to death. Sheriff Black is on his way, and needless to say we've got a crime scene here."

"And where in the hell is Peter Waverly?" Hunter said as he stroked a strand of hair away from Colette's forehead.

"Maybe we'll find something inside that will lead us to him," Greg said.

"We'll ransack the damned place until we find the connection," Nick replied.

"There's got to be something that will lead us to Peter," Barry added.

Hunter barely listened to the conversation. His sole concentration was on Colette. He stroked his fingers over her forehead, down her fevered face. Dear God, why wasn't she awake? What all had she endured in the hands of this madman? It appeared she had been beaten around her face—what injuries couldn't he see?

Thank God he heard the ambulance approaching, the siren screaming with urgency. He needed them to take her, to fix her. He needed to see her smile again. He needed, wanted to see the beautiful blue of her eyes again.

He didn't care whether she had loved him or used him. None of that mattered right now. He just wanted her to be okay. He wanted her to survive this horrendous ordeal and live to thrive.

Within fifteen minutes the ambulance screamed away from the scene with Hunter in hot pursuit. She had regained consciousness as they'd loaded her into the ambulance, although Hunter hadn't been able to speak to her.

It felt like déjà vu as he parked in the hospital lot and ran for the emergency waiting room. Once again Sandy Silver sat at the desk.

"I know why you're here, and I've already told Dr. Lockwood you would be here," she said sympathetically. "He'll be out to speak to you when he can."

Hunter gave a nod and then sat in one of the chairs. Once again he was alone in the waiting room. How badly had she been hurt by Hank? What had she endured in the couple of hours she'd been in captivity? What kind of horrible pain had she suffered?

Thank God Nick had shot Hank and not Hunter. It would make the investigation into Hank's death clean. Hunter just wished they had captured or killed Peter. As long as that man was out there, Colette would always be at risk.

She would probably go on the run again. An aching hollowness blew through him as he thought of never seeing her again.

Emily lied to deceive. Colette lied to save her and her daughter's lives. Nick's words repeated in Hunter's head. Everything she'd lied about had been for self-preservation from a man who wanted her dead. And

Hunter now understood what kind of sick monster she'd been running from.

How could he be angry with her for her lies? All he wanted…all he needed to know was if she'd lied about caring for him. She'd told him she loved him. Had that been a lie?

He wasn't confused about his feelings where she was concerned. He was just confused about hers for him. Not that it mattered. If she chose to run again, then she would just be a happy, yet hurting memory, like that of his son.

The main thing right now was how she was doing. He had no idea what kind of torture she might have suffered. Did she have internal injuries? He'd seen her wrists, bloody and raw, and he wanted to weep as he thought about her being tied up and struggling to get free.

As bad as the physical pain might have been, he couldn't imagine the mental pain she must have suffered. She had to have believed that she was going to die, that her ex-husband would then have custody of Melinda. Those thoughts must have tortured her.

He jumped up from his chair as Dr. Lockwood came out. "We meet again," Dr. Lockwood said.

"Unfortunately. How is she?"

"According to her, she was slapped a number of times and one of her cheeks is definitely bruised. She also told me that she took a hard blow to the head that rendered her unconscious. We did some X-rays and I don't see any permanent damage. We've cleaned up and wrapped her wrists, and we've drawn blood because she told us initially she was drugged. Still, she's alert and doing remarkably well given the circumstances. She's a very strong woman."

Hunter expelled a deep sigh of relief. "Can I see her?"

"Room 109."

Hunter raced down the hallway, his heart beating a quickened pace. He turned into the room and breathed another sigh of relief as he saw her sitting up in the bed. She smiled. "I'm not sure how you all found me, but thank God you did," she said.

Hunter sat in the chair next to her bed. "You can thank George. He was bringing me some plants and saw you being taken from the house. He let us know it was Hank Bridges that had kidnapped you. I'm just sorry that we didn't get Peter."

She looked at him in surprise. "I thought you all knew."

"Knew what?" He hated that one of her cheeks was a fiery red. He wanted to place his hand on it and draw away the redness and pain.

"Hank was Peter."

He looked at her in stunned surprise. "What?"

"Peter had a bunch of plastic surgery done to completely change his looks. That's why nobody saw Peter in town."

At that moment Nick walked into the room. He nodded at Hunter and then smiled at Colette. "How are you feeling?" he asked as he sat in the other chair next to the bed.

"Pretty banged up," she replied. "But I'm happy to be alive."

"Are you up to answering some questions?" Nick asked.

"Absolutely," she replied.

Nick was just as shocked as Hunter had been to learn that Hank was Peter. As Hunter listened to her tell about how Hank had gotten into the house, drugged her and then she'd awakened tied to a kitchen chair, he wanted to kill Hank all over again.

She told them about Peter slapping and hitting her. Hunter wanted to cry for the pain she had suffered and still suffered.

"He planned on feeding me to the pigs," she said. Her eyes darkened. "He fed Ted and Sheila to the pigs." She shuddered, obviously thinking of what could have happened to her.

"It's over now, Colette. Peter is dead, and he'll never bother you again," Nick said.

"Thank God he'll never kill another person," she replied. "He can spend his eternity in hell."

"That's for sure," Nick replied. He got to his feet. "I'm sure we'll have more questions for you as the investigation unfolds. You'll be around?"

"I'll be around," she replied.

"It's finally over," Hunter said to her once Nick had left the room.

"It is. I'm sad that Melinda will never have her father in her life, but she's better off not having Peter in her life," she replied.

"So what are you going to tell her about all this?"

"I'll tell her that Hank Bridges was a bad man who tried to hurt me. I really believe she's too young to burden with the truth about Peter. I'll tell her about her father someday when I feel like the time is right. In the meantime all she needs to know is her father stopped talking to her at night."

"That sounds like a good plan." He gazed at her for a long moment. "You're really free now, Colette. You're free to live your life on your terms. You can go anywhere you want, live whatever life you want."

"Nothing has changed for me. I still want to make Dusty Gulch my forever home." She gazed at him somberly. "I know you probably can't forgive me, Hunter." Her eyes filled with a sheen of tears. "I lied to you about so many things. But I swear I didn't lie to you about my feelings for you."

He searched her face…her beautiful but beat-up face. "You don't need me anymore, Colette. There's no more threat to you."

Her eyes widened and then narrowed. "Is that what you think? That I was only with you for some sort of protection? Oh Hunter, I was with you because I wanted to be. I was with you because I fell hopelessly in love with you. I want my future to be with you. I want to marry you and have your babies. I want you to be the father figure in Melinda's life. I desperately want to spend the rest of my life with you. None of that had anything to do with my fear of Peter." Tears began to race down her cheeks.

"Don't cry, Colette." He reached out and took one of her hands in his. The words she had just spoken caused happiness to flutter in his heart and shot a huge ray of sunshine into his soul.

"There's nothing for me to forgive. You lied to save your life. Colette, don't cry. I fell hopelessly in love with Ainsley, and I'm hopelessly, desperately in love with Colette. I want the same things you do. Will you marry me? Colette, will you be my wife?"

"Deputy Churchill, there you go seducing me again," she said.

"And I intend to seduce you every day for the rest of your life if you'll let me." His love for her nearly took his breath away.

"Nothing would make me happier." She began to cry once again. "But…but I have one more secret," she said through her tears.

Hunter steeled himself, wondering if everything was about to be exploded apart. "What's the secret?" he asked hesitantly.

"I'm really a blonde," she confessed.

Relief whooshed through him. "You know what's amazing? I love blondes. I especially love a blonde named Colette who is the strongest, most amazing woman I've ever met."

Her tears turned to laughter. "I love you, Hunter."

"I'd like to kiss you, but I'm afraid I might hurt you," he said.

She smiled. "My lips are the only thing on my face that doesn't hurt."

"Well, in that case…" He stood and bent over her and gently took her lips in a kiss that fed his very soul. "I can't wait for you to become Mrs. Hunter Churchill," he said when the kiss ended.

"The very worst day of my life has now turned into the very best day of my life," she said. "Kiss me again, Hunter."

"Gladly." The kiss he gave her held all the passion, all the love he had for her, and he knew theirs would be a love, a marriage that would last a lifetime.

* * * * *

Don't miss other suspenseful titles by Carla Cassidy:

Stalked in the Night
48 Hour Lockdown
Desperate Measures
Desperate Intentions
Desperate Strangers

Available from Harlequin Intrigue!

COMING NEXT MONTH FROM

H HARLEQUIN
INTRIGUE

Available March 30, 2021

#1989 THE SECRET SHE KEPT
A Badge of Courage Novel • by Rita Herron
A disturbed student made Kate McKendrick's high school a hunting ground. Now Kate's the school's principal, and she's working with former bad boy Riggs Benford to uncover the secrets of that day and help the town heal. But a vengeful individual will do anything to keep the truth hidden.

#1990 THE SETUP
A Kyra and Jake Investigation • by Carol Ericson
Detective Jake McAllister doesn't know Kyra Chase is connected to an unsolved murder. He only knows his new case partner is a distraction. But with the body count rising, they'll need to trust each other in order to catch a killer who seems to know more about Kyra than Jake does.

#1991 PRESUMED DEADLY
The Ranger Brigade: Rocky Mountain Manhunt • by Cindi Myers
Dane Trask will do anything to bring down a drug ring, but he knows his first step is getting Ranger Brigade officer Faith Martin's help. But when their investigation means eluding Faith's fellow cops *and* an unknown killer, will the rugged Colorado terrain help them...or ensure their demise?

#1992 THE SUSPECT
A Marshal Law Novel • by Nichole Severn
Remington Barton's failure to capture a murderer ruined her career as a sheriff. Now she's a US marshal—and a suspect in a homicide. Her ex, Deputy Marshal Dylan Cove, never stopped hunting for the killer who eluded her. Can they prove her innocence before they become the next victims?

#1993 PROTECTING HIS WITNESS
Heartland Heroes • by Julie Anne Lindsey
When her safe house is breached, Maisy Daniels runs to Blaze Winchester, the detective who didn't just investigate the murder of Maisy's sister. He's also the father of her soon-to-be-born child. Can Blaze stop the killer hell-bent on keeping Maisy from testifying?

#1994 K-9 COLD CASE
A K-9 Alaska Novel • by Elizabeth Heiter
With the help of his K-9 companion, FBI victim specialist Jax Diallo vows to help police chief Keara Hernandez end the attacks against their community. Evidence suggests the crimes are connected to her husband's unsolved murder. When bullets fly, Jax will risk everything to keep his partner safe.

YOU CAN FIND MORE INFORMATION ON UPCOMING HARLEQUIN TITLES, FREE EXCERPTS AND MORE AT HARLEQUIN.COM.

He'd recognize that voice anywhere, even though he'd
heard it live and in person just a few times and never
so…forceful. He believed her, but he had no intention
of letting her off the hook so easily.

He raised his hands. "I'm LAPD Detective
Jake McAllister. Are you all right?"

A sudden gust of wind carried her sigh down the trail
toward him.

"It…it's Kyra Chase. I'm sorry. I'm putting away my
weapon."

Lowering his hands, he said, "Is it okay for me to
move now?"

"Of course. I didn't realize… I thought you were…"

"The killer coming back to his dump site?" He flicked on the flashlight in his hand and continued down the trail, his shoes scuffing over dirt and pebbles. "He wouldn't do that—at least not so soon after the kill."

When he got within two feet of her, he skimmed the beam over her body, her dark clothing swallowing up the light until it reached her blond hair. "I didn't mean to scare you, but what are you doing here?"

"Probably the same thing you are." She hung on to the strap of her purse, her hand inches from the gun pocket.

"I'm the lead detective on the case, and I'm doing some follow-up investigation."

"Believe it or not, Detective, I have my own prep work that I like to do before meeting a victim's family. I want to have as much information as possible when talking to them. I'm sure you can understand that."

"Sure, I can. And call me Jake."

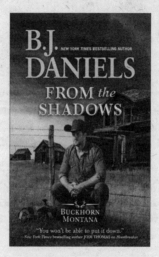

SPECIAL EXCERPT FROM

HQN

*Everyone says the hotel Casey Crenshaw inherited is
haunted. She wants to sell it as quickly as possible, but
Finn Faraday is throwing a wrench into her plans. He's
determined to figure out what happened at the hotel
years ago, but Finn and Casey will soon discover that
digging into the past can be dangerous...*

Read on for a sneak preview of From the Shadows,
*the second book in the Buckhorn, Montana series
by* New York Times *bestselling author B.J. Daniels.*

Chapter One

Finn lay on the dusty floor of the massive, old and allegedly
haunted Crenshaw Hotel and extended his arm as far as it
would go into the dark cubbyhole he'd discovered under the
back stairs. A spider web latched on to his hand, startling
him. He chuckled at how jumpy he was today as he shook
the clinging strands from his fingers. He had more to worry
about than a few cobwebs. Shifting to reach deeper, his
fingers brushed over what appeared to be a notebook stuck
in the very back.

Megan Broadhurst's missing diary? Had he finally gotten
lucky?

The air from the cubbyhole reeked of age and dust and
added to the rancid smell of his own sweat. He should have
been used to all of it by now. He'd spent the past few months
searching this monstrous old relic by day. At night, he'd lain
awake listening to its moans and groans, creaks and clanks, as

if the place were mocking him. *What are you really looking for? Justice? Or absolution?*

What he hadn't expected, though, was becoming invested in the history of the place and the people who'd owned it, especially the new owner—who would be arriving any day now to see the hotel demolished. Casey Crenshaw had inherited the place after her grandmother's recent death. Word was that she'd immediately put it up for sale to a buyer who planned to raze it.

Finn had been looking for a place to disappear when he'd heard about the hotel, which had been boarded up and empty for the past two years. He'd known it would be his last chance before the hotel was destroyed. It had felt like fate as he'd gotten off the bus in Buckhorn and pried his way into the Crenshaw. He'd been in awe of the hotel, which had once been popular with presidents, the rich and famous, and even royalty, the moment he stepped inside.

He'd only become more fascinated when he'd stumbled across Anna Crenshaw's journals. That was why he felt as if he already knew her granddaughter, Casey. He was looking forward to finally meeting her.

His fingers brushed over the notebook pages. He feared he would only push it farther back into the dark space or worse, that its pages would tear before he could get good purchase. Carefully he eased the notebook out.

This was the first thing he'd found that had been so well hidden. He hoped that meant it was the diary that not even the county marshal and all his deputies had been able to find.

Don't miss
From the Shadows *by B.J. Daniels,*
available March 2021 wherever HQN books
and ebooks are sold.

HQNBooks.com